# The Traveling Circus

# The Traveling Circus

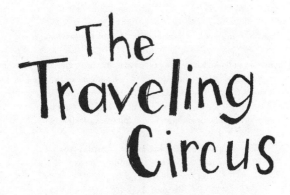

BY *Marie-Louise Gay*
AND *David Homel*

GROUNDWOOD BOOKS
HOUSE OF ANANSI PRESS
TORONTO   BERKELEY

Groundwood Books / House of Anansi Press
110 Spadina Avenue, Suite 801, Toronto, Ontario M5V 2K4
or c/o Publishers Group West
1700 Fourth Street, Berkeley CA 94710

We acknowledge for their financial support of our publishing program the Canada
Council for the Arts, the Government of Canada through the Canada Book Fund
(CBF) and the Ontario Arts Council

 **Canada Council** **Conseil des Arts**
**for the Arts** **du Canada**

 ONTARIO ARTS COUNCIL
CONSEIL DES ARTS DE L'ONTARIO
an Ontario government agency
un organisme du gouvernement de l'Ontario

Library and Archives Canada Cataloguing in Publication
Gay, Marie-Louise, author
The traveling circus / by Marie-Louise Gay and David Homel.
Issued in print and electronic formats.
ISBN 978-1-55498-420-6 (bound). — ISBN 978-1-55498-784-9 (html). —
ISBN 978-1-55498-785-6 (mobi)
I. Homel, David author  II. Title.
PS8563.A868T728 2015          jC813'.54          C2014-906794-1
C2014-906795-X

Groundwood Books is committed to protecting our natural environment. As part of
our efforts, the interior of this book is printed on paper that contains
100% post-consumer recycled fibers, is acid-free and is processed chlorine-free.

Design by Michael Solomon
Printed and bound in Canada

RECYCLED
Paper made from
recycled material
FSC® C103567

For our Serbo-Croatian friends

# My Adventures

## The Day Max Lost His Marbles!

$\mathcal{T}$his is how the trip began ...

The trip where we saw a church as big as an ocean liner, visited an island with no vowels, stumbled across a war-torn village and met the mysterious hermit of Vrgada. The trip where Max and I almost spent our vacation in prison, where we ate *krumpir* and *blitva*, but never saw the Leaning Tower of Pizza. The trip where Max got lost at least twice, almost drowned once and was nearly captured by a Minotaur.

It all started on a freezing winter's day — the day Max lost his marbles. I don't mean that he went crazy, though that happens pretty often.

Max had invented a game with our cat, Miro. It was very simple. Max would throw marbles all over the hardwood floor in the kitchen (for maximum noise and distance). Miro would pounce from the table, the counter or the top of the refrigerator and try to capture them. Meanwhile, Max would do the same thing. Whoever caught the most marbles won.

It was a game that demanded high intelligence and great skill.

Well, this time the stove won. Every single marble rolled under it. I had to lie flat on the floor and try to push out the marbles with my ruler.

On my third try, I fished out a postcard. (You've got mail!) There was a faded picture of a rocky island in the middle of a turquoise sea.

It was impossible to read the message. The writing looked like a bunch of crushed spiders.

But the picture on the postcard was great. You

could almost feel the sunshine beating down on the red roofs of the little stone houses.

Meanwhile, here in Montreal, the snow was piled up to the second-floor window — and I'm not exaggerating by much!

As if on cue, my parents came into the kitchen. They can smell a foreign place a mile away.

"Hey, that's the old postcard from Fred," my father said. "The one from K-r-k. I've always wanted to go to a place with no vowels."

"That's what you said when we got this card two years ago," my mother told him. "And we went to France instead."

"You want to go to K-r-k?" Max asked. "How could you go if you can't even say the name?"

"I'll learn!" my father answered.

When he starts getting his enthusiastic voice, and my mother gets her dreamy, faraway look, I get my familiar sinking feeling.

Another family trip to an impossible destination is on the horizon — this time to a place whose name no one can even pronounce.

My mother read the card out loud, but I think she was making the whole thing up. No one could read that squished-spider writing.

"*Dear Friends,*" she read. "*We are waiting for your visit. There's plenty of room for everyone. We'll take you to Vrgada, the island where Gordana was born. Meanwhile, here's a picture of Krk. She sends her love and so do I. Fred.*"

"Who's Fred?" Max asked.

"And who's Gordana?" I said.

"They're old friends of ours," my father said. "From a long time ago."

"They used to live in Yugoslavia," my mother explained. "But the country doesn't exist anymore."

If a country stops existing, where does it go? Does it just drop off the map? Or does the sea swallow it up like the lost continent of Atlantis?

And where do the people go? Do they escape in boats or on foot? Or do they wake up one morning and find out that they're living in a new country, with new food and different houses?

"Where do they live now?" I asked.

"After the war in Yugoslavia," said my father, sounding just like my hundred-year-old history teacher, "the country split into five new countries. One of them is Croatia. That's where Fred and Gordana live now."

Oh, boy! A country broken up by a war, where people spoke a language with no vowels, and that no one could understand. The perfect place for a vacation!

I don't know about you, but I didn't even know where Croatia was. Though I had the feeling I'd be finding out soon. I knew my parents. They just loved visiting a new country or discovering an out-of-the-way place.

Who knows what would have happened if Max hadn't lost his marbles that day?

Sure enough, the next week, when I came back from school, there was a book on the kitchen table. *Serbo-Croatian for Beginners.* I sighed.

I wasn't in the mood to learn another language. And I didn't want to go off on one of my parents' great escapes to nowhere.

How could I get out of this trip?

I went upstairs and told my brother that we had to figure out a plan to stop our parents from taking us on another crazy family vacation. Then I went to my room and closed the door.

The next minute, Max came bursting in.

"I know! We'll hide in the basement. We'll stock up on food and take the TV down there. They can go on their own!"

Poor Max. He actually thought our parents would abandon us just like that.

"Don't be silly," I told him. "They would never leave us alone."

"What if we stayed with Grandma?"

"They'd say she's too old to take care of us."

"Then we could take care of her," Max suggested. "When she loses her keys or her glasses or her shoes, I could find them for her."

I sighed. Then Max got another of his great ideas.

"I know," he said. "We could say we're allergic to the food there. We can't eat *krumpir*."

"What's that?"

"*Krumpir* means potatoes in Croatian. Everybody knows that."

"Sure, everybody. But nobody's allergic to potatoes." Then I looked at him again. "Have you been reading that book?"

"Well, kind of. I started at the back. There's a list of things to eat."

That's Max for you. The human vacuum cleaner.

"Couldn't you learn to say something better than potatoes? How about chocolate milkshake?"

"I didn't see anything about milkshakes in the book."

Just great, I thought. I was going to a country where there was nothing to eat but potatoes.

Since there didn't seem to be any way out of this trip, the next day, after reading the first pages of the language book, we decided to practice our extremely large vocabulary at the dinner table.

"*Ja sam Charlie,*" I said to my mother.

*"Ja sam Max,"* my brother said to Miro. *"Ja sam gladan."*

Then we burst out laughing. The words sure sounded strange.

My mother was happy. "That's great! We were afraid you boys wouldn't want to go on this trip."

"Who says we want to go?" I asked.

"But you're learning the language. That must mean you're willing to go."

As if we had any choice, I thought.

"We'll be able to count on you to talk to people over there," my father added. "Kids learn languages faster than adults."

Sometimes it was better not to know too much. I'd heard somewhere that a little knowledge could be a dangerous thing.

I turned to Max.

"Hey, what does *gladan* mean?"

"Hungry," he said.

Somehow I wasn't surprised. "You can order all the *krumpir* you want."

"What's a *krumpir?*" my father wanted to know.

"I can't tell you," I said. "It's secret Croatian code."

On Saturday afternoon I came back from playing hockey on the rink in the park. I was in a pretty bad mood. I didn't mind if our team lost, but the man who took care of the heated shed where we changed decided he wanted to go home. He put all our stuff outside and locked the door, and it snowed into my boots.

My father was sitting at the kitchen table with his favorite toy, which happened to be a map.

He looked up. He was so excited that his glasses nearly slipped off his face.

"Charlie! Did you know that the closest airport to Rijeka, in Croatia, where Fred lives, is Venice?"

I felt like saying, "So what?" My feet were like two ice cubes. I wanted to go to my room, shut the door, put my feet on the radiator and listen to some music. I wasn't in the mood to talk about next summer.

But my father was.

"We can fly to Venice, rent a car and drive the rest of the way. Doesn't that sound great?"

"Sure. Whatever you say."

Then Max bounded into the room with Miro sprinting after him.

"Italy!" he yelled. "Can we go on a gondola? Can we see the Leaning Tower of Pizza?"

Max has a one-track stomach.

"First of all, it's the Leaning Tower of Pisa," I told him. "And it's nowhere near Venice."

Max's face fell. I knew him. He had pictured a giant tower of cardboard boxes full of steaming-hot pizzas with all the toppings.

"Are we really going on this trip?" I asked my father.

"Of course," he said happily. "I'm buying the tickets tomorrow."

"Ya-ay!" Max yelled, as he and Miro galloped around the kitchen table.

My mother put her head in the doorway and smiled. At least one of their kids was enthusiastic about the trip: my brother, the traitor.

I went up to my room, slammed the door and lay down on the bed.

When would I get to decide what I did on vacation?

Never.

I plugged in my earphones and turned up the volume. Real loud.

# ONE
## *Lost and Found*

$\mathcal{S}$ix months later, there we were at the Venice airport after an all-night flight from Montreal. Airports are supposed to be air conditioned, but this one was as hot as a furnace.

I think we all looked like we had spent the night under a bridge. My father's hair was sticking up and his glasses were crooked. My mother's clothes were wrinkled and her eyes were bleary. Max was slung over my father's shoulder and he was snoring away loudly.

I couldn't stop yawning.

Sometimes I wonder why people want to travel. It can be so much effort!

On the plane, I decided I might as well find out what there was to see in Croatia, so I flipped through the guidebook.

In a place called Šibenik, a stone carver wanted to put some sculptures on the outside of a church. To do that he needed money, so he asked all the rich people for a contribution. Some of them refused, so to get his revenge, he carved sculptures of them and made them look like monkeys.

The sculptures are still there, and I bet their grandchildren are getting teased in school.

Of course, there are loads of castles and towns with walls around them. In a city called Split (like in banana split), an emperor built a palace entirely out of marble. It would be a great place for skateboarding.

But if I had a choice, I'd go cave diving, or wreck diving. I wondered if I could convince my parents to pay for the lessons.

I read about the huge walls around the city of Dubrovnik. They looked so big I bet you could drive a car on them.

The guidebook said that the wars were all in the past. But there were battles in Dubrovnik in 1991 and 1992.

That's not very long ago.

I found out another thing. The sides that were fighting then were the same ones that fought in

World War II. Fifty years later, they started up the same war.

Didn't they learn anything the first time?

As we drove out of the Venice airport in our rented car, my father was nervous. He was gripping the steering wheel very tightly, and I couldn't blame him. Honking cars and roaring trucks surrounded us on all sides. The drivers were changing lanes at top speed. It was like bumper cars at the amusement park, only for real.

Meanwhile, my mother was looking for her glasses so she could read the map.

When she got her hands on them, she told my father, "I think you should have gotten off at the last exit."

We hadn't been in Italy for an hour, and already we were lost.

My father never wants to admit he made a mistake, so very casually he announced, "Actually, I thought we would stay in Padua. It's just down the road from Venice."

"What about my gondolas?" Max demanded.

"There will be gondolas. Another time."

"What's in Padua?" I wanted to know.

"Your grandmother's favorite saint," my father told me. "Saint Anthony. He's the one who helps her find her glasses."

My mother gave my father one of her that's-enough looks. She doesn't like him making fun of my grandmother.

"People pray to Saint Anthony for all kinds of important things," my mother said. "Grandma does when she's not feeling well, and it works."

"I think it's just a superstition," my dad added. "Your grandmother has lots of them. You know, like not opening an umbrella indoors."

"Why would anyone want to do that?" Max asked. "It doesn't rain in the house."

"That's the point, Max," I told him. "It's a superstition. Opening an umbrella inside is supposed to give you bad luck."

"I could take Grandma a souvenir from Padua," my mother said. "She would love that. And they say it's a beautiful town."

"And much less crowded than Venice," my father said. "It will be easier to get around and park the car."

Of course, I thought. More off-the-beaten-track stuff. I should have known.

On we drove to see the saint who takes care of lost things. I hadn't lost anything yet, though I was about to lose my temper. That's because my brother was losing his mind again. He twisted and turned, but he couldn't go very far because he was pinned down by his seatbelt. He decided he wanted to look out my window, since he was sure the view was better on my side of the car.

"Hey, look!" he shouted, nearly poking out my eye. "Italian sheep! And Italian cows, look!"

He kicked me in the shin to get me to pay attention. When that didn't work, he started opening and closing his window. Every time, a burst of noisy, hot, exhaust-smelling air poured in from the highway.

My father blocked the power window switch. That didn't stop Max from exploring the wonders of an Italian car. He unbuckled his seatbelt, slid down to the floor and pulled the first lever he saw.

My mother's seat reclined — very fast. She didn't like having her head in the back seat.

"Why don't you take a nap?" she said to him. "You must be tired."

The wind had turned my mother's hair into a bird's nest. She had dark circles under her eyes. She was the one who needed a nap.

"What's on the radio?" Max wanted to know.

My father sighed and turned on the radio. Two announcers were talking away at top speed in Italian. They sounded very excited, as if their pants were on fire.

"Isn't there any music?" Max complained.

My father sighed harder. He hit a button on the radio. Rap music poured out of the speaker in Italian. I had no idea what they were saying. It rhymed, that's all I knew. Max started bouncing up and down to the beat, kicking the back of my mother's seat and punching the roof of the car.

I was dead tired from the plane trip. If Max wanted to listen to Italian rap, he could. Even with the racket from the radio, I closed my eyes and fell asleep.

When I opened my eyes, we were parked in front of a metal fence in the middle of a street. My parents were talking in Italian — a language they didn't speak — to a policeman who didn't have a gun. But he did have a very bushy mustache and matching eyebrows.

My parents were waving their guidebook with the names of the hotels in it, pretending to speak Italian. The policeman was waving his hands in the air, too, as if the book were a fly he was trying to chase away.

Max was fast asleep. Playing with the car windows must have worn him out.

In front of us lay a giant square full of people on bicycles. There wasn't a car in sight. At the far end of the square stood a church as big as a castle.

My parents must have figured, since they didn't speak Italian, that if they waved their hands in the air very hard and very fast, someone would understand them. People say that Italians talk with their hands. If you ask me, everyone does. I don't speak Italian, and I couldn't understand anything the policeman was saying, but one thing was clear.

We had come to a no-car zone.

What did my father say? Padua would be easier to get around in than Venice? Boy, was he wrong!

We piled out of the car as people on bikes went whizzing past. I saw businessmen in suits, their ties flapping in the wind, talking on their cellphones as they pedaled along. A girl my age was holding a pizza box in one hand like a waiter, and steering with the other. There were women wearing lots of makeup and high heels, smoking cigarettes and eating pastries — and riding at the same time.

A guy with a huge plant tied to his basket went past, followed by a girl with a birdcage strapped to the luggage carrier on her rear fender. The bird didn't look very happy.

The bicycles all looked like they belonged in a black-and-white movie. They had high straight handlebars, fat balloon tires, chain guards and baggage carriers tied on the back.

Nuns were riding slowly across the square, heading for the giant church. Their long black dresses flowed out behind them like sails. Their bikes had covers over the back tires to keep their dresses from getting tangled in the spokes.

My father started dragging the suitcases out of the trunk. The last piece of luggage was Max. My

father picked him up and set him on the hood of the car, where he went on sleeping.

Meanwhile, the policeman was pointing at the gigantic square. The hotel must have been out there somewhere, across the sea of cobblestones.

We started trudging in that direction.

My parents' suitcases bounced over the pavement, making a terrible racket. My backpack felt like it was full of rocks. Everyone who rode past stared at us, and some of them rang their bells impatiently.

It took forever to cross the square. I felt like I was in a dream where I was running to get somewhere, and that place kept getting farther away.

The closer I got, the more the church looked like a fortress, with thick walls and tall towers for pouring boiling oil down on the enemy, like in the Middle Ages. It was early morning, but crowds of people were streaming through the huge doors. It was like they were disappearing into a black hole.

Finally we reached the hotel: Casa del Pellegrino. A pellegrino, the hotel brochure explained, was a pilgrim.

Well, why not? I felt like I had just crossed the desert barefoot.

Max and I had just finished dragging our packs up to our room when the hugest racket I'd ever heard exploded in my ears. At first it sounded like cannons going off. Then I realized what it was.

Bells. Church bells. My mother probably wanted to get us a room inside the church, but she settled for the next best thing. Right across from it, facing the bell tower.

In the middle of all the noise, another bell went off. It was the phone.

A phone call? How could that be? I didn't know anyone here.

I picked it up.

"Isn't that the most beautiful sound you've ever heard?" Of course it was my mother. The same bells were ringing madly over the phone, like in stereo. "The bells of Saint Anthony of Padua!"

"Thanks for telling me," I said. "I never would have noticed."

A few minutes later, my mother marched my brother, my father and me up to the giant doors of the church. It was a beautiful warm day with a brilliant blue sky, and the first thing we do is disappear into a dark, clammy church. Does that make any sense to you?

On the way there, we passed dozens of tents and stalls where people were buying Saint Anthony souvenirs.

"You could get something for Grandma here," Max told my mother.

"Not yet. I'm looking for the perfect gift."

When my mother starts looking for something perfect, it can take forever. We could spend our whole vacation searching.

It took a while to get used to the dark church. We walked past paintings with candles burning in front of them. People were waiting in lines in front of little booths. Everyone was very quiet.

"What are they doing?" Max asked loudly.

"Shh! They're going to confession," my mother whispered.

"What's that?"

"That's when you tell your sins to a priest and he forgives you."

Max stopped and stared. I bet he was wondering what sins he could tell the priest. I could give him a few ideas.

Up ahead, the crowd was even thicker. The church was like the subway at rush hour.

"This is it," my mother whispered. "This is his tomb."

"Why is Mom whispering?" Max asked in his usual loud voice.

I elbowed him in the ribs, but not too hard.

"Everybody is whispering," I whispered. "Except you."

It was true. Everyone's voice was very low, as if they were telling secrets. And they were talking to a giant block of granite. *The Tomb of Saint Anthony* was written on the stone in just about every language in the world.

Some people were on their knees in front of the tomb. Others were resting their foreheads against it, as if they were asleep. Lots of people were kissing the stone.

We walked past a very large statue of Saint Anthony wearing a purple velvet cloak. People had taped photographs and pictures on the statue and dropped off secret messages on carefully folded pieces of paper.

"Those are messages to Saint Anthony, asking for help," my mother explained.

Then she took a little piece of paper from her purse and pinned it to the statue's robe.

"It's a message from Grandma."

I knew it! We hadn't accidentally missed the exit to Venice. We were going to Padua the whole time.

I wondered what message Grandma wanted us to deliver to Saint Anthony. Maybe she had lost her keys again.

The rest of the church wasn't nearly as crowded. The sun was shining through the stained-glass windows and making puddles of color on the floor. Pigeons were flying around under the giant domed ceiling. In a quiet corner, my father had found a free chair and fallen asleep. He was snoring but, luckily, not too loud.

My mother looked around. Then she tapped him on the shoulder.

"Where's Max?" she asked.

He opened his eyes wide and sat up straight, doing a bad job pretending that he hadn't been sleeping.

"I thought he was with you."

"I thought he was with you."

I should have known! The church was as big as an ocean liner and there were thousands of people moving in every direction. It was the perfect place for Max to get lost. Lost on purpose, so we would all have to go looking for him.

"When did you see him last?" my father asked my mother.

"I'm not sure. Just a minute ago."

My parents started looking behind the statues and pillars and all the other places where Max would never be.

It's not that hard to find Max. You just have to think like him. You have to creep into his mind and read his thoughts.

"Wait here," I told my parents. "I'll find him."

I went past the lines of people waiting to talk to Saint Anthony, but Max was nowhere to be seen.

Then I spotted a sign: *To the Crypt*. An arrow pointed downward.

A crypt like in *Tales from the Crypt*? Ah-ha! That was exactly the kind of place Max would want to see. I was beginning to think like Sherlock Holmes.

I slipped down the steps into a giant room. The air was dusty and cool, and the place had a strange empty feeling. Candles were burning in the four corners of the room. No one was there but me, even though, right above my head, thousands of visitors were crowding the church.

Did I say no one was there but me? Well, not quite. But I was the only *living* person in the crypt.

Right behind me — lying in a glass case, wearing a dark purple robe — was a skeleton. The skull seemed to grin, and its hollow eye sockets stared right at me.

I wasn't exactly scared. I was just a little ... nervous.

The skeleton must have been rich when he was alive. He was surrounded by all kinds of things made of gold and silver: vases, candleholders, bowls — you name it.

What a waste. He couldn't use those beautiful things anymore.

If Max came down here and saw that skeleton's grin, he wouldn't stay long. He'd be out the door in a second.

I didn't see a door, but I did see a second arrow. An arrow with a sign under it that read *Orto Botanico*. I had no idea what that meant, and neither would Max. But he would want to get out of the crypt in a hurry.

I followed the arrow, went down a dark passageway, pushed open a heavy iron door ...

And there I was, out in the sunshine again, in a
garden.

That was a relief! No skeletons were looking
over my shoulder. But I still hadn't found Max.

The *Orto Botanico*, it turned out, was a huge
garden. But there weren't any flowers or vegetables like in normal gardens. I saw rows and rows
of plants with signs nailed into the ground next to
them, and a skull and crossbones.

*Garden of Poisonous Plants*, the signs said in
three languages. I guess they didn't want to take a
chance that someone would munch on the plants.
They had enough skeletons already.

Maybe that's what happened to the skeleton
in the crypt. Someone fed him a poison salad. He
should have gone one row farther on, to where the
medicinal plants grew. Maybe there was an anti-
dote to poison salads there.

The poisonous plants had a gardener to match.

*"Benvenuto!"* a man shouted.

I wheeled around. A man with dark glasses and
a nose like a turnip was coming toward me with the
biggest, sharpest pair of clippers I'd ever seen.

He was wearing a long black cassock like a
priest, and it was stained green, probably from the
poisonous plants. Muddy rubber boots covered his

feet. He reached down and pulled a few leaves off a plant. He began to laugh, and his face creased into a million tiny lines. His mustache was yellow and so were his teeth.

"Belladonna!" he shouted. "You try?"

"No, thank you," I told him, trying to be polite, which is always a good idea when you're face to face with a crazy man holding enormous clippers and poison leaves.

I had gone from the frying pan into the fire. Or was that from the crypt into the poison garden?

I moved away slowly. Max wouldn't have stayed here either if he'd seen that man.

I went down the next row of plants as the man laughed and muttered to himself. But the next row wasn't much better.

*Garden of Thorns*, I read. There was a jumble

of angry-looking thistle plants, sticker bushes and cacti.

*Carnivorous Plants*, the next sign said. I saw cobra lilies, bladderwort and a Venus flytrap. Unfortunately, I didn't have any hamburger to feed it. I poked my finger into its mouth, and it snapped at me.

I spotted some people with guidebooks in their hands, looking at a four-hundred-year-old palm tree that had its own glass house. Most trees lived outside, but not this one. Maybe it was a dangerous tree, and that's why they kept it in a glass prison. That wouldn't have surprised me in a garden where you could get poisoned, eaten or seriously scratched.

But Max wasn't anywhere in the garden.

The Venus flytrap gave me an idea. Maybe it had given Max the same one. I decided to trust my detective's intuition.

I left the garden and headed onto the giant square that we had crossed with our baggage. A row of trees shaded the sidewalk.

Sure enough, under those trees was a gelato stand.

Gelato, in case you didn't know, is Italian for ice cream.

Max was standing there, staring at the tubs of ice cream under a glass case. He had this desperate look on his face.

That's because he had two big problems. He didn't speak Italian, and he didn't have any money.

I crept up behind him.

"Don't eat the belladonna ice cream. It's poisonous!"

He jumped a mile into the air.

"How did you find me?"

I wasn't going to tell him about my secret powers of deduction.

"We'd better go. Mom and Dad have been looking all over for you. Are you ever in trouble!"

A couple of minutes later, we were back inside the cool dark church. I didn't have any problem finding our parents. They were talking to a policeman again, and their arms were flying like windmills in a storm.

My mother saw us.

"Saint Anthony brought you back!" she cried.

She hugged Max so hard she almost strangled him. She was so happy, she forgot to be mad. Sometimes Max gets lucky.

"*Si, si, San Antonio,*" the policeman agreed.

Saint Anthony? More like Saint Charlie, the patron saint of detectives.

# TWO
## Pigs on Spits

The next day, everything went back to normal in Padua. Cars took over the main square that had been filled with bicycles the day before. The honking horns were nearly as loud as the church bells.

On the way back across the square, my mother stopped in front of a bakery window.

"Look, the perfect gift," she cried.

In the shop window, there were tiny models of the Saint Anthony church, with the garden of poisonous plants behind it and the square in front.

"You want to buy Grandma a model of the city?" Max asked.

My mother laughed. "It's made of marzipan."

"What's that?"

Max might not know what marzipan is, but I do. It's a dessert made of crushed almonds and loads of sugar, and you can make it in any color and shape you want.

We followed my mother inside. I wondered how she was going to buy an edible church without knowing Italian. But she was lucky. The baker had studied marzipan-making in Paris and spoke French, and so does my mother.

She chose two of everything: the church, the garden and all the buildings around the square, in different colors. Each one was no bigger than my finger. The baker wrapped everything up in tissue paper and put the candy buildings in a fancy box with a gold bow around it, as if we had just bought a diamond ring.

"Why did you buy two?" Max asked.

"Grandma can keep one as a souvenir and eat the other. You know how much she loves sweets."

My father let out a sigh of relief.

"Mission accomplished," he declared. "And in record time."

Max was practically drooling as we left the shop. I knew exactly what he was thinking.

"Whatever you do," I whispered, "don't even think about eating Grandma's church."

Our car was right where we'd left it, underneath a tree. The pigeons that had their nests in the branches must not have liked the color, and they decided to change it. The car was splashed and splattered with white and gray and green stuff — totally disgusting!

"Croatia, here we come!" my father announced as we piled into the car.

"Wait a minute," Max complained. "What about the gondolas? What about the Tower of Pizza?"

"We'll stop in Venice on the way back," my father promised.

Max slumped back in his seat and stuck out his bottom lip. He didn't believe my parents, and neither did I.

After an hour's drive, we crossed the border into another country. The first thing I saw was a pig on a spit turning over hot coals. The pig was moving fast. If he had been alive, he would have been really dizzy.

"Look at that!" Max shouted. "Do people really eat a whole pig for breakfast?"

In the next little town, I saw another one. Then another. The pigs were in little shelters that looked like bus stops. In case it rained, I guess. And the spits were motorized so they would move at just the right speed.

The cooking pigs were all turning in front of restaurants. It was early in the morning, but the chefs had already started cooking their pigs so they would be ready for lunch. Or maybe people liked to eat roast pork for breakfast in Slovenia.

That's right. Slovenia. There was a little sliver of that country between Italy and Croatia, where Fred lived. We weren't going to be in Slovenia for more than thirty minutes. I would get a new stamp in my passport to go with the usual history lesson from my father.

"Slovenia was one of the new countries that was formed when Yugoslavia broke up in 1991," he lectured, one hand on the wheel and the other in the air. My mother always gets nervous when he drives like that. "All the parts of the country wanted to be independent, and they started fighting each other. They didn't really stop until 1999."

"Why did they have to fight? Couldn't they have just shared the country?" I asked.

"Sometimes people are too mad to talk to each other," he said.

My brother looked out the window.

"I don't see any war here."

"If we're lucky, we won't see any anywhere we go," my father answered.

There were no signs of war, but Slovenia did look a little old and tired. The fancy four-lane highway in Italy was now a narrow two-lane road. In the towns we drove through, I didn't see any kids. Just adults sitting on painted wooden chairs in front of their houses, staring at us as we went by.

Maybe they were waiting for their pigs to cook.

I tried to read the signs, but I couldn't understand a single one. I was like someone who didn't know how to read. That felt really strange, as if I was cut off from the rest of the world.

Suddenly the road was blocked by an enormous traffic jam. My father hit the brakes and we stopped just in time behind a truck from Turkey.

"Now what?" my father wondered.

"Maybe we're at the border," my mother said. "It'll probably take a while."

We sat there for a few minutes in the middle of nowhere, with trucks in front and behind us. Standing in his field, a farmer who looked a hundred years old was leaning on his pitchfork, smiling. Maybe he was happy we were stalled behind a great line of trucks in front of his field, so he would have something to look at.

The next minute a car

pulled up next to us. It was stuffed full of people — six or eight of them — and they were waving their arms and shouting.

"*Avanti, avanti!*" they yelled. "Come on!"

They were telling us to follow them and pass the trucks, which is exactly what my father did.

"Wait a minute," my mother told him. "You're going to drive on the wrong side of the road and pass all these trucks? In a foreign country where you don't understand anything that anyone is saying?"

"That's illegal," my little brother pointed out.

"If that guy is doing it," my father reminded him, pointing to the car in front of us, "I can, too."

We followed the car jammed full of people, speeding past the trucks waiting in line. I figured if something dangerous was waiting up ahead, the other car would get to it first.

A minute later, we reached the border. Dozens of soldiers wearing uniforms like in a World War II movie were standing around. Some were carrying machine guns, and they had taken up position by the kind of gates you see at railroad crossings.

As the car in front of us went through, we waited quietly. Except for Max. He started twisting and turning on his seat.

"I have to go to the bathroom," he whined.

"Wait a while," my mother said.

"I can't hold it anymore."

I could feel my mother thinking. How long could Max last? Or was he only exaggerating?

I knew what would happen next.

"Charlie," she said. "Take him somewhere no one can see."

"Like behind a tree," my father added.

I knew that much.

"Come on, Max. Before you explode. Your eyes are starting to get yellow."

He shot out of the car. I took a look around. There was a guard post for the soldiers, and maybe they had a toilet. But their machine guns made me think twice.

I spotted a tree on the other side of the guard's house — a very big tree with bushes all around.

"This way, Max. No one will see you."

On our way back to the car, a soldier stepped in front of us.

*"Pasos."* He stuck out his hand. "Passport."

*"Ja sam Max,"* my brother said.

The soldier didn't smile. He wasn't impressed by Max's Croatian.

"In the car," I told him.

My parents popped out of the car like they were on springs. My mother came running toward us.

"Halt!" the soldier shouted.

He pointed at the ground, then drew a line in

the dirt with the toe of his boot. We all looked at the line.

"Slovenia," he said seriously, and pointed at my parents. "Croatia," he said, and pointed at Max and me. Then he frowned and shook his head.

"You've got to be kidding," my father said.

That was the wrong thing to say. The soldier made us stand right where we were. Max and I were on one side of the line. My parents, whom I could practically touch, had to stay on the other side, in another country. The soldier marched off to the guard post.

"Max," I whispered, "the next time you want to go to the bathroom, bring your passport."

He looked like he would burst into tears. My father gave me a dirty look. Okay, maybe it wasn't the best time to make a joke.

If Max cried, the soldiers might think something was really wrong. We would all end up in prison, or worse. What a vacation that would be!

The next minute, another soldier came strolling up to us. He was older and had more stripes on his uniform. He was smiling, but it wasn't a friendly smile. It was an I'm-going-to-eat-you-alive smile.

He pointed at Max and me.

"They have crossed into Croatia without passports. That is a crime."

"But they're just kids," my mother said.

"Passports," the soldier demanded.

My father went back to the car and came back with our four passports.

"Children's passports," the soldier ordered.

My father did what he was told. He handed the soldier our two passports.

The soldier looked at them.

"*Kanadska,*" he said.

It was now or never for our Croatian vocabulary.

"*Ja sam Charlie,*" I told him.

"*Ja sam Max,*" my brother chimed in.

"*To je dobro!* Good kids!"

· He gave us a friendlier smile this time. Then he handed Max and me our passports, and we were allowed to cross the line in the dirt to where our parents stood, two steps away.

I could feel my father trying very hard not to say something that would get us into trouble all over again.

We got back in the car and drove to the checkpoint a stone's throw away. There were more soldiers with more machine guns, pointed at the ground, which was a relief.

I saw why all the trucks were lined up on the road. They were waiting to cross the border at the truck checkpoint. At the car checkpoint, there was nobody but us.

At the border crossing, a man in a booth was waiting for us. He looked extremely bored, even if he did have a soccer game playing on a tiny television hidden under the counter.

He looked happy to see us, probably because no one came to visit him. He gathered up all our passports and read them front to back, then back to front.

*"Kanadska?"* he said to my father.

My father nodded. The guard shook his finger at him.

"No pee-pee in Croatia," he laughed, very happy with his joke. He stamped our passports. "Welcome!"

After a few more hairpin turns on the narrow road, I saw the sea sparkling in the morning sunshine far below. The water was silvery blue and the light was so strong it hurt my eyes. Islands were scattered along the coastline like Max's marbles.

"Which one is K-r-k?" I asked.

"I don't know, but aren't they beautiful?"

I knew my mother was going to say that. She had forgotten all about how Max and I were nearly thrown in prison.

Sometimes my parents just didn't take things seriously. I mean, how would they have explained that to our friends back home, and especially to my grandmother? "Oh, we had to leave the boys in a prison in Croatia. But don't worry, they'll be out in a couple of years."

We went down the side of a mountain, weaving our way behind the heavy trucks spewing black smoke. My mother was slowly turning green, which usually happens on roads like this.

We drove into a long, dark tunnel. Half the lights were out, and other cars were speeding past us with no headlights. When we finally came out alive, I spotted the sign for Rijeka.

"Fred told us to get off at the first exit," my father said.

"It's about time," my mother groaned. "I've had enough of this road. Then what do we do?"

My dad took a note out of his shirt pocket. "We drive up the hill, and you can't miss it," he read.

"Those are the instructions to Fred's apartment? I can't believe it. Let me read that."

"That's what he wrote," my father admitted. "You can't miss it."

In all my travels, there's one thing I've learned. When someone says You can't miss it, you know you'll never find the place in a thousand years.

"It's on Budinicova Street," my mother read.

"There you go," my father smiled. "That's a start."

It would have been a start in any other place. But not here. None of the streets had signs. All the streets could have been Budinicova. Or none of them.

We drove up a hill covered in apartment buildings that all looked the same: worn out and tired, with gray concrete faces stained by rusty water. They were four or five stories high and had crumbling concrete balconies.

"We'll have to ask someone," my mother decided.

*"Ja sam Max,"* my brother declared.

"That's a big help," I told him. "We know you're Max, but we don't know where we are."

I got out my Croatian dictionary and started searching for helpful words. Somebody had to do something.

Meanwhile, my father parked, and we got out to stretch our legs. An old man came walking slowly down the street. He was smoking a bitten-down pipe and had a dog as old as he was.

The man must have lived here forever. If anyone knew where Budinicova Street was, he would.

He gave us a suspicious look when he spotted the foreign license plates on our fancy rented car.

*"Gdje je Budinicova?"* I asked.

I hoped that meant, "Where is Budinicova?" But I wasn't too sure.

The man looked at me like I was a Martian. Then he blew a puff of smoke from his pipe, turned and started walking the other way. His wrinkled old

dog stared at us for a moment, barked once, then followed him.

I guess I hadn't said the words right, or maybe people didn't like foreigners here.

"I can't believe you didn't get better directions from Fred," my mother told my father. She shook her head. "You can't miss it," she said in a sarcastic voice.

There must be some way of finding Fred's house. I looked up and down the street with no name, but there wasn't anyone to ask for help. A few people passed by on motor scooters. I tried to flag them down, but they just waved and kept going.

"We'll just stand here," my mother declared, "until someone asks us if we need help."

"You could always try Saint Anthony," my father suggested.

"This is no time for your jokes," my mother told him.

Then, from far above, I heard a distant voice.

"Hey, down there! Look up! This way!"

We looked up in the air. On a balcony high above, a man was waving his arms like a sailor who has spotted land after months at sea.

"It's Fred!" my father shouted.

"You're late!" Fred called down. "What happened to you? Wait — I'm coming down!"

"See, I told you," my father said happily. "You can't miss his place. I knew it."

Right, I thought. It was just a lucky break. Or maybe Saint Anthony after all.

A few minutes later, a tall man with a long gray beard and a wide smile came out of the building. His skin was very dark, as if he had spent his whole life outdoors.

"Welcome to Croatia!" he shouted. He gave my father a huge bear hug.

Then it was my mother's turn. After that, he hugged Max and me together, though we had never met him before. It was like a reunion of long-lost friends who didn't know each other.

"Libero's waiting to meet you," he said to me. "Let's go up."

Libero?

Fred showed my father where to park — right on the sidewalk. If cars parked on the sidewalk, then people walked in the street. Everything was opposite here.

Once our bags were in a heap in the middle of the road, and the car was parked half on the sidewalk, half on the street at a crazy angle, Fred folded in the side-view mirror so no one would hit it.

Then we started lugging our bags up five floors to Fred's apartment.

"Sorry," said Fred. "The elevator isn't running today. Actually, it hasn't run since last year."

Streets with no names. Suspicious people with suspicious dogs. Elevators that never worked.

You get the picture?

I couldn't tell whether Fred's apartment was small, or whether there were too many people in it who were too happy to meet me. Maybe I was just tired after the trip, but I couldn't keep anyone's name straight.

That's because they all had the same name.

When we walked in the door, a woman rushed to greet us. She was holding a spatula in her hand.

"I am Gordana, Slobodan's wife. So very happy to meet you!" she said to Max and me. "I feel I know you already."

She bent down and gave Max a big kiss. A drop of oil slid off her spatula onto his head. He didn't notice, so I guess it wasn't boiling oil.

"Wait, I thought your name was Fred," I told Fred.

Before he could answer, a small bald man, the exact opposite of Fred, shook my hand.

"I am Slobodan. Very happy to meet you. I have heard so much about you."

A guy my age took his place. He held out his hand.

"Hello, Charlie. Pleased to meet you. I am Slobodan."

What kind of place was this? The streets had no names, but the people all had the same name.

"Are you sure your name isn't Slobodan, too?" I asked Fred's wife.

She laughed and waved her spatula in the air like she was conducting an orchestra.

"Don't be silly! That's a name for boys. But you are right, there are a lot of Slobodans here. So they had to take different names. That one," she said, pointing to her husband, "is Fred. And the other one without the hair is Bobo. And the youngest who has been waiting to meet you, he's Libero."

That didn't make much sense. But I kept that thought to myself and asked another question instead.

"How come the streets don't have names?"

"They're changing them. They took down the old names two years ago, but they haven't put up new ones yet."

"The government can't agree on what names they should use," Fred told me. "So everyone gets lost. That's why I was watching out for you."

"What does Budinicova mean?" I asked.

"He was a hero from World War II."

"Why did he lose his street?"

Fred shrugged. "When there's a new country, you get new heroes. That's the way it is."

He didn't look very happy. Maybe Mr. Budinicova was a friend of his.

Libero, Max and I went out on the balcony. It was like an extremely small backyard, five floors up in the sky. There was a barbecue, but no pig. Tomatoes and red pepper plants and something that looked like spinach were growing in pots. Clotheslines heavy with laundry crisscrossed above our heads. Part of the balcony was covered in grape vines that had climbed up from the balcony one floor down.

"How did you get the name Libero?" I asked. "It doesn't sound very much like Slobodan."

"Fred's my grandfather, and I'm named for him. So I'm Slobodan, too. It means freedom in Croatian. But since I live in Italy, everyone calls me Libero."

"Which means freedom," I figured, "in Italian."

"I'm going to change my name to Slobodan, too," Max announced.

"We have enough of them already," I told him. "Try something different, like *krumpir*."

Libero burst out laughing. "That's a good name for him!"

I could tell that Libero and I were going to get along.

The adults came out. I sure hoped the balcony was strong enough to hold all of us.

"That's where we're going," Fred said, pointing out to the sea. "As soon as Gordana finishes the picnic."

"Are we going to K-r-k?" Max asked. "The place with no vowels?"

"Actually, we're going to C-r-e-s," Fred told us. "I have a friend who has a little house there."

"How little?" I asked. I could just imagine us all jammed into the same room.

"You'll see," Libero said. "It's really tiny but there are beaches and forests and all sorts of things to do."

This trip might not be so bad after all, I thought.

Suddenly Gordana rushed into the apartment. Smoke was coming from the kitchen.

She had left her wooden spatula in the frying pan.

Fred ran in after her and threw water on the pan. Steam and smoke filled the kitchen. They both came back onto the balcony, coughing, tears streaming down their faces.

At least we didn't have to call the fire department.

# THREE
## Close Calls

*A*fter Gordana rescued her burning spatula and stowed our meal in her enormous picnic basket, we lugged our bags down the stairs again and tried to put everything back in the car.

How hard can it be to leave on a car trip? You throw your bags in the trunk and drive away, right? Especially when you have two cars.

Wrong.

First you have to stand around and talk about the trip for hours. It's like putting together a jigsaw puzzle. Only the pieces are people and luggage.

"Our friends need a guide," Bobo said to Fred and Gordana. "So you should ride with them."

"The picnic basket won't fit in their trunk," Gordana pointed out.

"I need room for my wife Silvia," Bobo answered. "She always packs an enormous suitcase. And she has to be in the front or she'll get carsick."

I knew that trick. My mother always said that so she could get the best seat in the car.

We stood around in the middle of the street, trying to decide who would take which car, who would sit in which seat and who would get more carsick. We spent so much time figuring it out that people stuck their heads out their windows and started giving us advice.

"Put all the suitcases in one car," an old lady with purple hair yelled. "And stuff the kids in the trunk!"

The adults all laughed like crazy.

Grown-ups have a strange sense of humor, no matter what country they are in.

Max, Libero and I played street soccer with a stone and tried not to get too bored.

A half hour later, the Traveling Circus got on the road. At this rate, we'd never get anywhere.

When you're really tired, you can sleep through nearly anything, including a car full of adults squawking like parrots.

The next thing I knew, Fred was tapping me on the shoulder.

I opened my eyes. We were on a bridge.

"Welcome to K-r-k!" Fred announced.

"Nice," I said, and closed my eyes again.

I woke up a few minutes later. We were in front of the water. K-r-k turned out to be not much bigger than the postcard Fred sent us.

"Stop by the dock," Fred told my father.

We got out of the car. There was a small dock and a stretch of water with another island on the other side. I spotted a ferryboat in the distance. It didn't look big enough to carry two cars.

"How are we going to get across?" Max asked.

"We'll swim," I told him, "and use our backpacks as life preservers."

Max looked worried as Fred got on his cellphone.

"We won't be leaving right away," he announced after his conversation. "The ferryboat man is having lunch. It'll be a while. Usually he takes a nap afterward."

"What do we do now?" My father looked almost as worried as Max.

Fred's phone rang. After a few words, he told us, "No problem. Here comes the picnic."

Bobo pulled up in a cloud of dust. Libero and Gordana jumped out of the back seat and got the picnic basket from the trunk.

From the front seat, very slowly, Bobo's wife appeared. She looked like a movie star. She was wearing a big floppy hat and enormous sunglasses that covered most of her face. Her long yellow dress blew like a flag in the wind.

Bobo introduced us. "This is my wife, Silvia."

She shook our hands but didn't take off her sunglasses.

"Sorry, I don't speak English," she said.

"Yes, you do," Max told her. "You just did."

"Stop that, Max. You can say *Ja sam* Max, but that doesn't mean you know Croatian," my mother told him. I think she was embarrassed, and a little impressed by Bobo's wife, who was putting on more lipstick.

With her bird's-nest hair, T-shirt and sandals, my mother sure didn't look like a movie star.

Gordana spread out a blanket on the grass by the water.

"If it's lunchtime for the captain, it is lunchtime for us, too," she said.

She opened her gigantic picnic basket. Wrapped in foil with newspaper around it was the meat she had been frying. I guess it didn't burn after all.

"You must taste my famous car-trip chicken recipe."

It smelled great, especially since we hadn't eaten anything since breakfast in Italy. All those pigs on spits had made me hungry.

Her picnic basket was bottomless as well as gigantic. She took out jars of roasted red peppers, marinated onions and smoked fish. There was a stew of *blitva* and *krumpir*. The *blitva* looked like boiled seaweed, but it tasted great. I looked it up in the dictionary. It was a kind of spinach. My vocabulary was growing with every meal.

I was starting to sound like Max, the human vacuum cleaner. But when you were waiting for a ferry to show up, eating made the time go by faster.

After lunch, we all took a nap on the picnic blanket because we were too full to do anything else.

The sound of the ferry horn woke me up. I got to my feet and watched as the boat slowly floated toward us. It was no more than a platform with a ramp on each end for the cars.

The captain looked like he had just woken up, too. From his spot on the bridge, he was yawning and drinking coffee out of a glass, and his white captain's hat was on backwards.

Once he docked, he came down. He and Fred hugged each other like long-lost friends who hadn't seen each other for centuries.

I guess that was how people said hello in this country.

We started to cross the narrow channel, with

the ferry vibrating and shaking and making a total racket. Up ahead, red cliffs rose out of the water. The island we were going to looked like a fortress.

Libero and I took turns looking through my father's binoculars. At first I thought the birds were flying straight into the cliff. Then I spotted the tiny holes where they had built their nests. Those birds must have had built-in radar!

Bobo was standing next to us. He pointed to the cliffs ahead.

"That's Cres, our destination."

I showed him the small island off in the distance.

"What's that place?"

"Goli Otok — the Bald Island."

It was just as bald as Bobo. I wondered if he noticed the resemblance.

Nothing was growing there but rocks. A big building with no windows stood in the middle of the island.

"What's in that building?" I asked.

"People. It's a prison." He paused. "I was there once."

I didn't know what to say. I'd never met anyone who had been in prison before. I wondered what Bobo had done. Was he a gangster or a murderer? He sure didn't look like one.

My brother, who had been spying on our conversation, burst out, "Why? What did you do? Are you a criminal?"

Max couldn't help himself. He had to say the first thing that came into his head, in a very loud voice.

Bobo laughed. "A criminal? No, I was in an auto accident."

"You went to prison because of an accident?" I asked.

"The other driver hit someone and killed him. Then he ran into me. Too bad for me. The driver was very high up in the government. A very important man. The police couldn't blame him, so they blamed me. Government orders. I had to go to prison."

"That's not fair!" my brother said.

"No, it's not," Bobo agreed. "But they sent me to Goli Otok anyway. No one can escape the island."

"Like Alcatraz," I said.

"Exactly. But without the Birdman." Bobo laughed. "But in the end, I flew away. The man stopped being so important. He ended up in jail, and I'm free now."

For someone who went to prison for something he hadn't done, Bobo sure smiled a lot.

I wondered why a government would put someone in jail when he hadn't done anything. Maybe that only happened in countries that had been through wars.

Meanwhile, Fred and the ferry captain were talking away on the bridge. I guess the boat knew where to go, because the captain was hardly paying attention. He had finished his coffee, and it had woken him up. He was pointing this way and that, and Fred was doing the same thing. They must have been talking about something very exciting.

We churned along toward Cres. My mother was standing at the railing in front, taking pictures of the island. Gordana and Silvia were in back, speaking softly and looking very serious.

Then, from the left side of the boat, I heard a *putt-putt-putt* sound. I turned and looked. A fishing boat was coming right into our path.

The captain hadn't even seen it. He was too busy swapping stories with Fred.

The cliffs of Cres were slowly drawing closer. But we'd never get there if I didn't do something fast.

I ran up the stairs to the captain's post on the bridge. I grabbed Fred's arm and pointed at the fishing boat that was sailing right into our path.

Fred's eyes grew very wide. He yelled something to the captain. The captain's eyes grew twice as wide as Fred's. He pulled on the ship's horn, and my eardrums nearly burst. Then he cut the engine and

fired the retro-rockets, or whatever car ferries big enough for two cars use. We slowed down, and the fishing boat sailed past, right in front of us, without a care in the world.

That was a close call!

"Why didn't he stop?" I yelled.

"The smaller vessel has the right of way," Fred explained. "It's the law of the sea." He watched the boat disappear into the distance. "You saved the ship and all hands, Charlie, not to mention the cars. Good thing someone was paying attention!"

He patted me on the shoulder and shook his finger in the captain's face.

We made it to Cres without anything else happening. When we docked and my father and Bobo drove the cars carefully off the ferry, the captain came over to me. He stood at attention and saluted. Then he stuck out his enormous hand and shook mine.

"*Hvala,*" he said. "Thank you very much."

Then he shook my hand some more.

Cres, in spite of the way it was spelled, was pronounced like "stress." Fred had told us that, and I saw why.

It had to do with the roads.

I'd been on a lot of narrow winding roads before, but nothing compared to Cres. On one side, there was a mountain that rose up to the sky. On the other side, there was a cliff that made your head spin, and that dropped straight into the sea.

Of course there was no guardrail.

All of a sudden, my mother didn't think that the beautiful blue water was so beautiful anymore.

"Stay on the road!" she told my father.

"That's my plan," he answered.

"Don't look down!"

"You shouldn't be looking down."

Fred was smart enough not to say anything. He must have been on this road dozens of times.

Then Max got into the act. The carsick act.

*Act One.*

"I don't feel very well," he complained.

"Close your eyes. We'll be there soon," my father said.

That didn't make sense. My father had never been here before. He had no idea when we would get there.

"I don't feel very well," Max repeated. "I think I'm going to be sick."

*Act Two.*

"Pull over!" my mother ordered my father.

"There's nowhere to pull over to."

Just then, a battered old rusty bus passed us on a curve, honking its horn and leaving us in a cloud of dust and flying gravel that bounced off the windshield.

*Act Three: The Glorious Finale!*

My mother turned and opened the door on Max's side — barely in time.

So much for Gordana's famous car-trip chicken!

Just then Fred's cellphone went off. He grabbed it.

"*Da ... da.*" He looked worried. "That was Bobo. Pull over as far as you can."

Luckily, we were on the mountain side of the road, and not the endless-drop-with-no-guardrail side.

The next minute, as my mother was cleaning

up Max, an enormous truck swept past. It took up nearly the whole road. There was just room enough for us to hug the rocky side of the mountain.

The truck was carrying pigs. Hundreds of squealing pigs that didn't seem to be enjoying the ride either.

Fred's cellphone rang again.

"We can go now," he told us. "It's clear sailing."

"Maybe for you," my mother said under her breath.

Bobo was like a scout for explorers on the wild frontier, warning of the dangers ahead. He used a cellphone instead of sending smoke signals.

Unfortunately, he didn't see everything.

Like the goats.

Just as we were entering our hundredth hairpin turn, my father slammed on the brakes. We all went flying forward.

A herd of goats was blocking the road. They were happily chomping away on the grass and weeds that grew up through the cracks in the cement.

When the goats saw us in the middle of the narrow road, a few feet from the edge of the cliff, they looked very happy. Ever seen a smiling goat?

"I know these goats!" Fred exclaimed.

"You know them personally?" my mother asked.

"I do," he said. "They're Branko's goats. That

means we're almost at Branko's house. Another few curves, and it's down to his place."

"Straight down?" my mother asked.

"Can you ask these goats to get out of the way since you know them so well?" my father asked.

Fred climbed out of the car and started bawling out the goats in Croatian. Very reluctantly, they moved out of the way. One of them went right to the edge of the cliff and looked down, a million kilometers to the sea.

"Look at that one," my father told my mother. "He's not afraid of heights."

"He's a goat," she answered. "Not a person."

My mother did have a point. They were called mountain goats for a good reason.

Branko, who owned the goats and the house where we'd be staying, had a face like a bull's, with dark leathery skin and crooked teeth. Pretty scary, except for his smile.

"Branko Vukmirovitch!" he shouted at me. Then he stuck out his hand. It was the size of a dinner plate.

I had to shake it. But I knew what was going to happen.

And it did. He crushed my hand to powder. Then he slapped me on the shoulder. Luckily, my backpack protected me.

"*Dobro sine!*" he shouted.

I had no idea what that meant, but I smiled anyway.

Everyone was the same here. They were all really happy to see each other, and they showed how happy they were by crushing each other with bear hugs and monster handshakes. When Branko tried to do the same with Max, my brother ran and hid behind my mother, who had already been bear-hugged.

Then Branko stopped in front of Silvia. She put out her hand like a real movie star, and he kissed it. He even blushed.

Branko loved flowers as much as he did turning people's hands into powder. The house was covered in purple and pink flowering vines, and flowerpots lined the porch.

"Oh, bougainvillea!" my mother exclaimed.

*"Da, da!"* Branko shouted happily at the top of his lungs.

I guess that flower had the same name in Croatian as in English. That was convenient, but it didn't add up to much of a conversation. Branko picked one of the purple flowers and gave it to my mother, who put it behind her ear.

"Let's move in!" Fred declared.

But first, Branko wanted to show us his kingdom. We visited the yard that had a picnic table with vines growing over it. The yard was a little like Fred's balcony, but five times bigger. Next to the table, of course, stood a giant fireplace for roasting large animals on a spit. On the other side of the house, sheep munched on the grass, and chickens fought over worms. At the far end of the driveway was the sea.

Fred said something to Branko, who burst out in a giant explosion of laughter.

"He always keeps his goats on the road," Fred explained. "They make people slow down before the last big hill. Otherwise, half the time they crash into his house or drive straight into the water."

He pointed to the seashore.

"Branko wants to show you his yacht."

Very proudly, Branko led us to the shore. A large wooden rowboat lay on the rocky beach. The boat was painted different shades of blue, and a rusty anchor kept the waves from carrying it out to sea.

A long conversation followed. Branko waved his hands toward the water. Fred pointed to Max and me. Bobo shook his finger at Branko. His wife Silvia crossed her arms and nodded.

"What are they saying?" Max asked.

I didn't know much Croatian, but even I could tell what was going on. Branko was inviting us out on his boat. Fred wanted to go, but Bobo would have nothing to do with it. And Silvia agreed with him.

I could see why. The inside of the boat was covered with layers of thick, stinky, oily tar to keep the water out. That didn't bother me, but I couldn't imagine Bobo's wife sailing away in Branko's "yacht."

When we carried our bags into the house, I saw why Branko was in no hurry to show us the inside. The house was all outside and no inside. The porch was great, and so was the yard, but there was one room for Max, Libero and me, and that was the living room. The adults would be walking past our heads, day and night. It would be like sleeping in a train station. No privacy at all.

Libero read my mind.

"That's the way it is here," he said. "On vacations, you're supposed to be close to people."

Close? I'd practically be in their pockets.

# FOUR
## *Fish Thieves!*

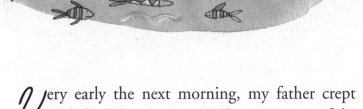

*V*ery early the next morning, my father crept into the living room to wake us up to go fishing. He was half-asleep himself.

"Let's go, you two," he whispered.

"What about Libero?" I asked.

"There's not enough room in the boat for everyone. But don't worry. He's been out fishing plenty of times."

Fred and Branko were waiting on the front porch with cups of steaming coffee and thick slices of bread. Fred handed me one. The bread was almost black. Maybe it was made out of charcoal.

That didn't bother Max. He wolfed his slice

down without bothering to chew it. The human vacuum cleaner strikes again!

On the table, I saw a bottle of clear liquid with something floating in it. That something looked like seaweed.

I blinked my eyes and looked again.

It wasn't seaweed. There was a snake in the bottle!

Branko picked up the bottle and poured three small glasses for himself, Fred and my father. Luckily, he didn't offer Max and me any.

My father raised his glass and gave me his here-goes-nothing look.

I couldn't believe he was going to drink it. What if the snake was still alive? I would have made sure it was dead. But not my father.

As soon as he swallowed the stuff, his face nearly turned inside out. He clapped his hand over his mouth to keep from coughing.

Meanwhile, Fred and Branko were slapping each other on the back as if they had just won the Stanley Cup.

It was a kind of contest. Who could drink snake juice at six o'clock in the morning and survive?

Breakfast in Croatia — at your own risk!

Down on the rocky beach, we pushed and pulled the heavy wooden boat over the rocks toward the water. Strips of tar were hanging from the bottom of the boat.

"Do you think this thing is safe?" Max whispered.

"Don't worry," I told him. "The sea is calm, and Branko probably goes out on the water every day."

Max still had his worried look as we climbed into the boat that, by the way, had no life jackets. But maybe the oars would float.

Branko took off his shirt, sat down at the oars and started rowing us out to sea. He was very large and pretty hairy. It was like going fishing with a bear.

As he rowed, Fred started to sing in a loud, croaking voice. Branko joined in. Between the two of them, they were going to scare away every fish in the sea.

When they had finished, Fred told me, "That was a fishing song. It brings you luck."

My mother would have liked it here, listening to the fishing songs and being out on the calm, blue-green water. But women weren't allowed on boats, Fred told me, even if all boats were named for women. Fishermen thought they brought bad luck. If a woman was on board, Fred said, there was sure to be a huge storm with enormous waves, or a whale would swallow up the rowboat like in *Moby Dick*.

If you ask me, that was just another superstition, like not opening your umbrella indoors.

It turned out we weren't really going fishing.

Branko rowed us to the spot where he had dropped his nets the evening before, where small plastic buoys were bobbing in the water. Gulls started gathering in the sky above us, hoping for a free meal.

"Start pulling up the nets," Fred said.

My father, Max and I grabbed the nets, while Branko sat on the other side of the boat so it wouldn't tip too far in our direction.

"Heave-ho!" Fred shouted.

Meanwhile, Branko sat smoking his pipe and smiling. He was happy that we were doing all the work for him.

"I wonder what we'll catch," Max said.

"Maybe a shark," I told him.

He dropped the net. "A shark?"

Fred laughed. "Not too many sharks here. We want to catch something for dinner."

I never imagined fishing could be so hard. The nets ate up my hands in no time. The cord was rough and gave me blisters, and the salt water stung my skin.

The net was too heavy for Max, but he didn't want to give up. He leaned over the edge of the boat to grab the net. He was huffing and puffing and his face was red.

The next thing I knew, there was a large splash. And it wasn't a shark.

Max had fallen head over heels into the half-submerged net. He was splashing and spluttering like a baby dogfish.

Of course, he wasn't in any danger since he was too tangled up in the net.

"Man overboard!" Fred shouted.

"I think we caught a big one!" I yelled.

Max was dog-paddling furiously.

"That's not funny," he cried. "Help me out!"

I leaned over the side of the boat, and my father grabbed the back of my pants so I wouldn't end up like Max. I held onto my brother's hand and pulled.

Maybe it was because he was waterlogged, but he weighed a ton. Fred had to help me.

"Heave-ho!" my father called.

Finally we got Max into the boat, where he landed like a fish out of water.

Meanwhile, Branko was blowing puffs of smoke from his pipe and watching the scene calmly.

"What should we do with the drunken sailor?" Fred sang.

"I am not a drunken sailor!" Max insisted.

No, I thought. A real sailor wouldn't fall out of a rowboat into a fishing net.

Max pulled himself onto the seat. He was a soggy mess. He pretended to be fascinated by the seagulls circling above, but I knew he was totally embarrassed.

We finished hauling the nets into the boat. I got ready to grab the fish. I knew they would be slippery and fast.

I leaned over, and that's when I saw it.

The nets were completely empty. There wasn't a single fish in them.

"Someone cut the nets!" Fred shouted.

He held up a length of the net. When Branko saw how it had been slashed, he slammed the oars into place and started rowing furiously back to land, muttering under his breath. I didn't need a dictionary to figure out what he was saying.

"Who do you think did that?" my father asked Fred.

"Branko is having a war with his neighbor. This isn't the first time someone has stolen his fish."

"Can't he call the police?"

"That would only make things worse. It's not so simple here."

Then I remembered Bobo's story about going to prison, and I figured that Fred had a point.

Libero was waiting for us on the shore. He had our snorkel masks and our beach shoes in a bag. As we climbed a steep bluff, I told him that the only fish we'd caught was Max, and that the nets had been cut.

"It was a fish thief," Max explained.

"Branko and his neighbor have been fighting for years," Libero said.

"About fish?" Max asked.

"No. About politics."

"Someone would steal his fish because of politics?"

"That's the way it is here," Libero said. "Neighbors can be enemies because their great-great-grandfathers had a little quarrel a hundred years ago. People never forget anything around here. They're like elephants. And their long memories keep the fighting going. That's why I live in Italy now. My parents couldn't stand it anymore."

My mother always said that holding a grudge just made you miserable. I guess no one knew that expression in Croatia.

We scrambled down the rough path to a little bay. The beach was made of shiny rocks of every shape and size. There wasn't a grain of sand anywhere. No wonder Libero had brought our shoes.

Three girls were lying on air mattresses. When we came close to them, Libero said something in Croatian. The girls giggled and answered.

"What are they saying?" I asked him.

"No idea. I think they're speaking Slovak, but I'm not sure."

"Do you speak English?" I asked the girls.

"Leetle beet," one of them said. Then she held

her finger and thumb up to show how little she spoke. An ant couldn't have slipped through the space.

The girls laughed, jumped up and dove into the water. Libero and I followed. Max decided he wanted to dry off before he went swimming again, so he had a stone-skipping contest with himself.

We put on our snorkel masks and swam past the girls. The water was so clear I could see the whiskers on the fish swimming beneath me. I surfaced and tried talking to the girls, but it was hard to talk and swim at the same time, especially when I didn't know the language. I tried French and Spanish and Libero tried Italian, but they just laughed.

There were just too many languages in this part of the world. It would be easier if everyone spoke the same one, but which would it be?

We gave up and went back to snorkeling. Beneath us there were fish of every size and color, from angelfish to needlefish, from neon blue to bright yellow and black.

I wondered how the fish communicated. Did they speak the same language? Or maybe they weren't on speaking terms, like Branko and his neighbor.

When my skin was as wrinkled as a prune, I swam back to shore. Libero picked his way over the rocks to the end of the beach. I followed with Max on my heels. The beach ended at a cliff, and we climbed it.

When we were sure the girls were looking in our direction, Libero said, "Watch this."

"Are you sure?" The cliff looked pretty high to me.

He dove in. The next thing I knew, he had surfaced at the foot of the cliff.

"It's safe," he called. "I do it every time I come here."

I took a deep breath. It was a long way down. I aimed for the spot next to Libero, and the water rushed over me. A few seconds later, I was swimming alongside him.

Of course Max didn't want to be left out. He climbed part way up the cliff, then threw himself off in a terrible bellyflop.

*Splash!* He hit the water stomach first. The girls laughed like crazy. He got their attention, all right.

Meanwhile, three guys showed up on the beach. Libero and I watched as the girls swam back to shore, grabbed their air mattresses and left. They waved and called out to us.

"I wonder what they're saying," I said to Libero.

"Who knows? Maybe better luck next time?"

We decided to head back to the house. We went up one side of the bluff and down the other and found ourselves in the little woods behind Branko's place. His rooster was crowing, even though dawn was long past.

Suddenly we heard voices.

Libero put his finger over his mouth, and we hid behind a tree. A minute later, we saw Fred and Branko walking quickly through the woods.

Suspiciously quickly, the Sherlock Holmes in me thought.

I saw another suspicious thing, too. The large cloth bag in Fred's hand was dripping water.

He and Branko were laughing and talking loud.

I turned to Libero. His eyes were wide.

A minute later, the two men disappeared among the trees.

"What were they saying?" I asked.

"I can't believe it! They stole back the fish!"

"How did they do that?"

"They snuck into the neighbor's house while he was having a nap, opened his refrigerator and took the fish. They said they could even hear him snoring!"

What a place. Grown-ups stealing each other's food!

"No one would ever do that where I live," I told Libero.

"This is a special island," he said, shaking his head.

"At least we'll have something for dinner," Max pointed out.

At the end of the afternoon, the fire was going in the outdoor fireplace and the table was set. I had never seen a table like this one. It was made out of stone, and moss was growing on it underneath the plates and glasses, like a living tablecloth.

"I have to take a picture!" my mother said, and she rushed off to get her camera.

Gordana was taking food off the grill and piling it on the table. There were plates of charred red peppers and zucchinis and tomatoes. She hadn't barbecued the salad, but she did decorate it with flowers from Branko's garden.

Fred rubbed his hands together when she brought the fish.

"It's a gilthead sea bream," he told us. "The best fish in the sea. It's sacred to Aphrodite."

"Who's that?" I asked.

"The Greek goddess of love and beauty."

I looked at the wrinkled, blackened fish and wondered what the goddess of love and beauty could see in it. Fred and Gordana posed with the fish as my mother photographed them. Then it was our turn. Max made rabbit ears behind the fish's head. Then everyone put flowers in their hair so we would match Gordana's salad.

It was the official Traveling Circus photo.

"Max," Libero whispered. "Don't say anything about where they got the fish."

Max didn't care where his food came from, as long as there was enough of it.

But it wasn't Max we had to worry about.

"Where did this fish come from?" my father asked.

Fred looked at Branko. Branko looked away, and then suddenly had a coughing fit. Both men burst out laughing, but they didn't answer.

My father looked confused. But, for once, he didn't totally embarrass me by asking more questions.

In no time, there was nothing left of the fish but the skeleton and the head.

"Charlie," Fred said to me very seriously, "you're missing the best part."

Like a surgeon, Fred took his knife and made

a cut just below the fish's eye. Very delicately, he took out a tiny bit of fish meat with the tip of his knife.

"Fish cheeks," he declared, holding up a small piece of meat as if it were a diamond. "They're the best."

Before I could think of a way of getting out of eating a fish cheek, he swallowed it down. Another close call!

When Fred went to get the bottle with the snake in it, Libero said to me, "I've got *Spaceballs* on DVD, but I don't get all the jokes. Do you want to look at it and tell me what everything means?"

We went into the house, with Max tagging along behind.

Libero learned English in school, but some things you can't get from books. Every time there was a joke he didn't understand, Libero stopped the film and asked me to explain. That's not the best way to watch a movie, but I didn't mind. I had seen *Spaceballs* so many times I knew it by heart.

When we got to the joke about Colonel Sandurz, Libero hit Pause.

"Is he a soldier? I don't get it."

There weren't any fried chicken restaurants in this part of the world, so I explained who Colonel Sanders was, and what it meant when you said that someone was chicken. There was plenty of pizza in Croatia, but no Pizza Huts, so I told him about those, too.

Libero understood, but he didn't laugh. I guess you just can't explain jokes.

And that's when everything went dark. Not just the DVD. The whole house.

"It happens all the time," Libero said. "The electricity goes off whenever it wants to."

We crept carefully into the kitchen in search of a flashlight.

"I hear music," I said. "How can that be?"

"We'd better investigate."

"Wait for me!" Max called, stumbling through the darkness.

We stepped onto the porch. The cooking fire was still smoldering, but no one was there. A candle was burning inside a small lantern. I picked it up.

The music was coming from farther away.

We went down the stairs and past the stone table. The air smelled of grilled fish. We left the yard behind, and darkness swallowed us up.

"Follow me," Libero said.

We passed Branko's house. There was no moon, and the stars didn't give much light. I couldn't see anything, but I could feel stones beneath my shoes. We were on the driveway that ran past a field where we had left the cars.

I saw goat shadows chewing on the bushes. We passed a line of trees.

All of a sudden the music got louder, and a strong light blinded me.

I couldn't believe my eyes.

There was our car, parked in the field with a few goats standing around staring at it. All four doors were open. Music was pouring out of the sound system, and in the headlights, I saw my parents, Fred and Gordana and Bobo and Silvia. They were dancing in the field to the music from the car's CD player.

Fred was whirling around in the headlights with Gordana. For an old guy, he could really dance.

I couldn't say the same about my parents. They kept tripping over the clods of dirt and molehills in the field.

The strangest-looking dancer was Bobo. He was jumping up and down in time to the music and pounding his chest with his fists like King Kong in that old movie. Meanwhile, Silvia looked at him from behind her sunglasses and shook her head.

"They've gone nuts," Max said, worried. "We'd better do something!"

"The snake bit them," Libero answered. "There's nothing to do but join them."

We walked into the glare of the headlights and started dancing to the beat. We weren't very good, but I didn't care. Our shadows were as tall as giants on the ground in front of us.

Suddenly, other shadows started dancing with us.

I couldn't believe it. The girls from Slovakia had come to our party.

And you know what I discovered?

You don't need to speak the same language to communicate with people when you're dancing in car headlights to Croatian music.

After a week on Cres, it was time to pack our bags and head for the next island, Vrgada. That was where Gordana was born, and where Fred had promised us we would go in his postcard I found under the stove, which started this whole Traveling Circus in the first place.

But first we needed to have another big goodbye scene and play musical chairs with our car seats again.

Unfortunately, Libero had to go back to his parents in Italy. Bobo and Silvia would drive him, and go to work afterward.

"It won't be as much fun without you," I told

Libero. "Who will tell me what's going on if you're not here?"

"You'll have to guess," he said. "Good luck."

We didn't know whether to give each other a big bear hug the way they did in Croatia, or just shake hands. So we did both.

I was sad as I watched him get into the car with Bobo and Silvia.

"I'll come back and visit you," I promised.

"Maybe I'll come and visit you first."

And then he drove away.

One good thing about traveling is that you meet all sorts of people, and some of them become your friends, like Libero. The only problem is that you have to leave them, sooner or later.

I promised myself that I really would come back and visit Libero.

I turned around and there was my family and Fred and Gordana standing around, studying our little car like it was a jigsaw puzzle they had to figure out.

My mother slid into the front seat. "If I don't sit here, I'll get carsick."

"I have to sit in front," my father added quickly, "since I'm driving."

"I want to be in front!" Max wailed. "Otherwise I'll get sick, too."

"No, you won't," Gordana told Max. "I'll tell

you a story about where we're going, and you'll forget to be sick."

My mother got the spot she wanted, but she had to share it with Gordana's giant picnic basket. There wasn't room for it in the trunk with our bags. It was so crowded in the back with all four of us that Max and I didn't even have enough room to fight.

We started up the mountainside on the twisty road.

"No throwing up allowed," I reminded Max.

"I can throw up if I want to," he said. "You can't tell me what to do."

"That's just the kind of conversation we don't need," my mother told us.

"Now we are going to the Dalmatian coast," Gordana told Max.

"Dalmatians?" he cried. "Like those dogs?"

"Exactly," I said. "Everyone who lives there is white with black spots."

"Actually," Fred said, "they're black with white spots."

"Like me!" Gordana said happily. "Because that's where I'm from."

Max looked at her. His eyes narrowed. I could see the little wheels going around in his head. Did Gordana really have black and white spots? Was that why she was wearing a long-sleeved shirt?

But he was afraid to ask.

By the time he was finished thinking about it, and sneaking looks at Gordana when he thought she couldn't see him, we had gone up and down the mountains and along the cliffs. He forgot all about being sick.

Gordana's trick had worked!

This time, when we took the ferry, the captain kept his eyes open. I didn't have to save the ship again. We reached the mainland where the road was flat and straight, but we still couldn't go very fast. There was always a tractor driven by an old lady in an apron, or a man wobbling down the middle of the road on an ancient bicycle.

The island of Vrgada was just a little farther down the coast, but it was taking all day to get there.

After a couple of hours, my father said, "I've had enough of driving. I say we take a break."

We pulled off the main road at the next little town. The main street was so rough that my head hit the ceiling of the car with every bump. The street was made for horses, or maybe tractors, but certainly not for cars.

We stopped in front of a church in a little square with willow trees. My father got out and immediately started doing his toe-touching exercises. I hoped no one was watching.

I did see two skinny cats curled up in the church

doorway. They stared at my father, then yawned and stretched to show him how to do it.

My mother started taking pictures of the cats, as if we didn't have any in Montreal. Maybe she was planning to show the photos to Miro so he could see what a good life he had with us.

Gordana rummaged in the picnic basket for some snacks for Max. A minute later, he had inhaled everything.

"Let's go exploring," he begged me.

"Go ahead," I said. "Just don't get lost."

I knew Max would get lost on purpose, the way he always does. He jumped up and ran toward the church, scaring the cats. He pulled on the door, but it was locked.

A few seconds later, he was back.

"There's no one home," he complained.

"Take a walk with Max," my mother told me. "But be back in five minutes."

"It's your summer job," my father said.

Very funny. If I got paid for looking after Max, I'd be rich enough to buy a car we could all fit into.

We walked past the church and into the village. The place was deserted, like a ghost town. Maybe the people were working in the fields, but somehow I didn't think so. The houses were shut tight, as if no one lived in them anymore. There weren't even any birds.

I was starting to get a creepy feeling as we went past an old wooden barn. We came to a street where the pavement was all broken up. On the other side of the street, every house was wrecked.

The roofs were caved in and the windows smashed. The walls were blackened by fire and some of the houses had giant holes blown in them.

Inside, they were empty, as if someone had stolen the furniture — even the pictures off the walls.

"What happened?" Max whispered.

He took a step toward a ruined house. I held him back.

"Don't. Look at that."

A sign hung sideways from a broken tree in front of the house: *Pazi — Mine / Danger — Mines.* A skull and crossbones made the message clear.

"Coal mines?" Max asked. "I don't see any."

"These mines are bombs hidden in the ground. They explode if you step on one."

Max froze, and didn't move.

Half the houses in the village were in perfect shape, and half were in ruins. And the whole place was completely empty.

Then I understood. This was the war.

"Let's go get Fred," I told Max.

We ran back to the car. My parents and Fred

and Gordana were sitting in the shade on a bench
in front of the church. They were laughing and telling stories, as if everything was perfect.

"I want to show you something," I told Fred.

My parents looked at us. Just like that, they
stood up. Sometimes they can read our faces. If
mine was like Max's, it was as white as a ghost.

They followed me through the empty village.

Everything was quiet except for the distant sound of a tractor going down the road.

"What happened?" my mother asked.

I didn't know how to tell her. She'd see soon enough.

When we came to the street that divided the town in half, my parents stopped in their tracks, the way we had.

No one said anything for the longest time.

"I heard about this happening," Fred told us after a while. "People being killed and chased away by their neighbors. I guess I didn't want to believe it."

"I always told you it was true," Gordana said. She was practically shaking with anger. "Now you have to believe it."

"Where is everyone?" I asked. "The whole village is empty. What about the people who live in the houses that are still standing?"

Fred pointed at the burned houses.

"They were forced to leave, even though they'd lived here all their lives. Who knows where they are now?"

He turned and pointed to the part of the village that was in perfect shape.

"They were thrown out by those people."

"But they're not here anymore, either," I said.

"They left because they were ashamed," Gordana told me.

Then I noticed words written in spray paint on the wall of a burned house.

"What does it say?"

"I can't tell you," Fred answered. Then he thought a little. "Yes, I can. But I don't want to. I'm sorry."

We walked back in silence and got into the car. Next to me, Fred and Gordana sat like two statues and stared into space. They didn't want to talk about what we'd seen, so I didn't ask questions, though I had plenty of them.

I wondered why people would declare war on their neighbors after they had been living together forever. What would it be like to live in a place like that?

I thought about my own neighborhood. On my street, people came from all kinds of different places, and they spoke different languages, and no one fought. What had gone wrong in this little village where neighbors had become enemies?

No one had won this war. One side lost their houses and had to leave. The other side left, too, because they were ashamed of what they had done.

There was nothing left but an empty village full of land mines, where no one could live.

An hour later, we were back on the coast again, driving along the seaside. As usual, Fred had a plan. We would leave the car in his friend Whitey's barnyard.

Then we'd take the ferry to Vrgada, where another house was waiting for us.

"There was no war in Vrgada," Gordana promised as we pulled into a farmyard full of goats.

"No," Fred added. "But Whitey had his share of troubles."

"Please, no more about the war," Gordana told him.

"What happened?" Max stared out the window. "Will we have to watch out for land mines?"

"Don't worry about that," Fred said. "Since Whitey didn't want to fight in the war, he left. When he came back, his neighbors had stolen everything out of his house — even the lightbulbs from the lamps. But afterward, everyone went back to being friends again."

"How could they?" my father wondered.

"They had no choice. They have to work together."

A man came out of the house to greet us. I knew he must be Whitey, since he had a big pile of white hair that looked like Dairy Queen ice cream. Or maybe his name came from the goats he kept. All of them had white fur.

In no time, dozens of goats had surrounded us. I'm not afraid of goats — not like Max. It's the flies I don't like. Every goat was accompanied by a thousand buzzing flies.

We ran for his house and slammed the screen door shut. It turned out we had arrived just in time for a goat-cheese tasting. We couldn't refuse, since that would have been impolite. In this country, when someone wants you to eat something, you're not allowed to say no. Not even to snake juice.

Whitey set out the cheeses on plates and chased away the flies that had invaded the kitchen in spite of the screens.

Fred did his best to translate for us, which couldn't have been easy.

"This cheese is made from goats that ate rosemary bushes." He pointed at a triangular cheese. "And this one is made from goats that ate clover."

"Yuck, that one's covered in dirt," Max said.

"That's not dirt. It's ashes. It helps preserve the cheese," Fred explained.

"Do ashes taste better than dirt?"

"Don't eat any," I told Max. "There'll be more for me."

Mrs. Whitey put food on the table: fruit, sausages, loaves of bread, bottles of wine and juice — enough for a dozen people. My mother patted the empty chair next to her, but she shook her head and disappeared into the kitchen.

"Dig in. You never know where your next meal is coming from," my father told me, goat-cheese crumbs flying from his mouth.

That was enough to kill anyone's appetite!

When we were so stuffed we could hardly walk, it was time to go. The goats were waiting to ambush us, but Whitey swatted at them with a broom. We pulled ourselves up onto the back of a flatbed truck. A flatbed is like a pick-up truck, only with no sides. Gordana sat on the picnic basket so it wouldn't slide off.

A few minutes later, we were at the ferry dock.

And I thought the ferry to Cres was small! This one was no more than a motorboat with an awning on top.

Of course Fred and Gordana knew the captain of the boat — if motorboats can have captains.

After they got through hugging and kissing and slapping each other on the back, Gordana said, "The captain is my cousin."

"Everyone is your cousin here," Fred laughed.

"Of course!" Gordana threw her arms open wide and laughed. "I am the queen of Vrgada!" She gave Max a sly look. "The queen of black-and-white spots!"

The captain started up the motor. It was about as powerful as a lawn-mower engine. Then he separated the women and the men, and Max and me, and made us sit on opposite sides of the boat. He divided the bags into two piles and separated them, too. I think he was trying to balance the weight so the boat wouldn't tip over.

My mother looked around for the life jackets.
There weren't any, of course. She held Max's hand
tightly, as if that would save him from drowning if
the boat capsized.

We managed to sail to Vrgada without sinking.
The trip took fifteen minutes. Fifteen minutes of
roaring engine noise and black, stinky smoke.

From a distance, the island looked like a camel
with a half dozen humps. Each one was a different
hill. The tallest had a church on top, and at the foot
of it was a town. The island was so small it could fit
into my pocket. I wondered what I would do there.

The captain piloted us into a bay where a few
fishing boats were tied up. They were no bigger
than Branko's rowboat, and patched with tar just
like his. The captain rammed the boat into some
old truck tires that were tied to the wooden pier,
and my teeth shook in my mouth.

No wonder the boats always needed to be
patched!

A man on the dock wound the rope around a
pole to keep us from drifting away.

Mission accomplished. We were in Vrgada.

Now what?

Something was missing, and I couldn't quite put
my finger on it.

Then I realized there wasn't a single car or truck
or tractor.

There wasn't even a road.

I jumped out of the boat and looked down the dock. You'll never guess what I saw.

An army of old ladies was moving in our direction. And they were all pushing wheelbarrows!

When they reached us, they crowded around Gordana, hugging her and chattering away at a thousand miles an hour. Then they grabbed our bags and started throwing them into their wheelbarrows. Max tried to hold onto his pack, but it was no use. The women were too strong. One of them gave him a big toothless smile as she grabbed his knapsack right out of his hands.

I guess they were the Vrgada Welcome Wagon

and the public transportation system all rolled up in one.

Laughing and talking away, the women began pushing their wheelbarrows loaded with our bags, Gordana's picnic basket and everything else we owned down the dock and onto the main street. Gordana led the way. She really was the queen of Vrgada.

Five or six extremely skinny cats and one three-legged dog trailed behind. It was a pretty strange parade. A few people opened their shutters to watch us go by.

The Traveling Circus had arrived!

When the wheelbarrow ladies stopped in front of our house, Max grabbed his knapsack. Did he think one of the ladies would run off with it? Who would want to steal his stuffed penguin and his precious plastic worm collection? Or his dirty socks?

"How much should I pay them?" my father asked Fred, reaching for his money.

"Put that away! They'd be offended if you tried to pay. They're all Gordana's cousins, or aunts, or both. I've never figured out who's who here. Except everyone is her family."

The ladies started carrying our bags into the house. Max and I followed them.

You know that expression, making yourself at home? That's what the wheelbarrow ladies were doing — in our house. They opened Fred and Gordana's little suitcase and began hanging their clothes in the closet. They took the food out of the picnic basket and stored it in the refrigerator. A lady came in with a bouquet of flowers and a plate of figs and arranged them on the table in the main room.

"Come on, Max," I said. "We'd better act fast. Otherwise we'll end up sleeping in the living room again."

We quickly explored the house and found two small bedrooms. One of the rooms had two single beds. I would have to share a room with Max, but that would be better than sleeping in the middle of the living-room floor.

Actually, what I really wanted was to have some time by myself. Back home, I could always go upstairs, close my door and shut out the world. When you traveled with your family, you were part of a flock of sheep. Everyone followed the leader, and they all stuck together.

I went back outside, with Max following me, of course. The adults had disappeared, but they hadn't gone far. In front of the village store, right next door, Fred and Gordana were sitting on two straight-backed chairs like the king and the queen on their thrones. They were surrounded by old men wearing sailor caps, who were holding onto their canes as if the first gust of wind would topple them over.

My parents were sitting on folding chairs, pretending they could understand what was going on. They definitely didn't fit in on the main street of Vrgada.

One reason was that my mother had pulled out her notebook and was busy sketching. I looked over her shoulder. She was drawing the cats that were sprawled every which way in the street, one on top of the other, in heaps.

Meanwhile, my father was reading the guidebook. He looked up.

"I don't get it," he said. "Vrgada isn't even in this book."

"Let me see." I took the guidebook from him. "Here it is! 'Vrgada, a tiny, sleepy island with no cars, where nothing ever happens. May cause a severe case of boredom.'"

"What?" said my father. "I didn't see that."

He took back the book. He read the page two or three times before he realized I'd made that up. It was so easy to fool him.

For such a tiny, sleepy place, there was a lot of action on the street, though it depends what you think is action. Another boat had pulled in, and the old ladies, wearing flowered scarves on their heads, were pushing wheelbarrows full of every possible thing up the street. Suitcases, firewood, potatoes, even kids. One woman was pushing a small refrigerator and another a wheelbarrow full of sandals. Going the other way, down the street toward the harbor, other ladies were pushing wheelbarrows filled with figs.

They weren't exactly pushing them. They were hanging on with all their might so the wheelbarrows wouldn't run away from them, since the street was so steep.

All of the people doing the work, I noticed, were women. And all of the people drinking coffee in front of the village store, I noticed, were men.

"Don't the men here work?" I asked Fred, who was drinking a coffee.

"Only women are allowed to drive wheelbarrows. Men do the important things, like thinking."

With Fred, you could never tell if he was joking.

"Why don't they use donkeys to carry things? They can walk on stones with no problem."

"Good question, Charlie. But that's a long story."

"I think we have time for it," I told him. What else was there to do?

He put down his coffee cup. He drank ten cups of coffee a day, and he never got nervous. But my father's hand was shaking from the one cup he had drunk.

"It's a long story, and a true one, too," Fred began. "One day, someone had the same great idea you did."

"I bet it was a woman who was tired of working."

"Who knows?" said Fred. "But someone thought, why should we be pushing these heavy wheelbarrows all day? We'll bring in a donkey to do the work."

"That makes sense."

"So the first donkey to ever set hooves on Vrgada comes across on a boat. That was a few years ago. I remember because I took the same boat. The donkey got seasick. It was terrible! Once he got here, people put him out in a field to calm him down. But he jumped over the fence and found some kind of plant that wasn't good for him. I have no idea what it was. He must have eaten a lot, because he

went completely crazy. The donkey turned into a lion. First he bit someone on the ear. Then he ran wild through the town, down this very street. People spent all day trying to lasso him with a rope. They tried tempting him with carrots, but he wouldn't have anything to do with it."

"Did they ever catch him?"

"Finally someone threw a blanket over his head, and the donkey stopped dead in his tracks. They put him back on the next boat. No one even says the word donkey on Vrgada, let alone invite another one over."

"I don't believe it," Max said. "A donkey can't turn into a lion."

But I believed Fred. It was a great story. He had loads of them, and I could listen to him all day.

Unfortunately, he went back to chatting with the toothless old men blowing smoke out of their pipes.

Since it wasn't too exciting to watch adults sitting around and talking in a language you didn't understand, I said to Max, "Let's go have a look around."

"Don't get lost," my father said.

Lost, on this tiny island? Impossible!

"And don't get hit by a wheelbarrow," my mother added.

We walked down the street to where the fishing boats were tied up. Men were crouching on the wooden dock repairing their nets.

So men did work here after all.

They looked up as we walked by, but they didn't say anything. They probably knew everything about us already.

"Hey, look at all those cats!" Max called.

There were even more cats here than on the street in front of our house. They were lying on the edge of the dock, staring at the water. Perched on top of old walls, basking in the sun. On window ledges and in doorways — hundreds of them!

Then I saw why. At the edge of the dock, fishermen were cleaning their catch. They were throwing the parts of the fish they didn't want in a heap next to them.

But the cats weren't serving themselves. They didn't have to. A woman was scooping up all the heads and tails and fish insides. She divided them into equal servings and put them on plates and saucers. Then she delivered them to the cats, wherever they happened to be, on the dock or the street or in front of the houses.

The old woman was like a pizza delivery guy, except with fish parts.

"This is cat paradise," said Max. "I can't wait to tell Miro about it."

"Just don't mention the smell," I told him.

He watched the woman as she did her errands, putting saucers of fish in front of cats.

"She looks strange," Max said.

He was right. She was big, with wild scraggly hair. Her mouth hung open, and I could see she had about two teeth.

She sounded strange, too. You know how people talk to their pets? Instead of talking, she made high-pitched squeaks like a bird.

"She's scary," Max whispered.

"She's not going to hurt you."

"What if she's a witch?"

As we walked past her, Max looked very hard at the ground. Maybe he thought she would turn him into a catfish if their eyes met. I didn't look at her, either, but only because it wasn't polite to stare.

After we went by, I turned around and snuck a peek. She was too busy with her cats to notice me.

"Don't worry, Max," I told him. "You're safe."

He stopped. He tried to do his spy imitation, and look at her out of the corner of his eye, but he wasn't very good at it.

The lady caught him staring. She started waving her arms in the air and cawing like a crow.

Max took off running as fast as he could.

I realized the woman couldn't talk. She could only make noises. And she really didn't like people staring at her.

I didn't blame her. I wouldn't like it, either.

I caught up to Max at the end of the dock.

"This place is creepy," he complained. "Why did we come here?"

"We have strange people back home, too," I reminded him. "Remember Tony the Ax Murderer?"

"Very funny."

Max turned his back on me and sulked. Tony the Ax Murderer didn't really exist. He was the old guy who drove the knife-sharpening truck through our neighborhood in the summer. Max convinced himself that he was a dangerous criminal because he had pictures of knives and axes on the side of his truck. Like the cat lady, Tony didn't like being spied on, either.

"I thought you liked cats. You could send Miro a postcard. I'm sure he'd like to hear about this place."

Whenever Max is in a bad mood, I can always cheer him up by talking about Miro.

"I'm going to do that!" he told me. "I bet they have postcards in that store."

I can never joke with Max. He always takes everything seriously.

Suddenly he had to send a postcard right away. We had to go back to the café next to our house. Of course, nothing had changed. Fred and Gordana were still surrounded by an admiring crowd. And my parents were still pretending they understood what was going on.

My mother had stopped sketching cats, so Max had no trouble talking her into buying him a postcard.

We went into the store. It was the size of a closet and filled to the ceiling with all sorts of strange things: clocks, tools, fishing equipment, rubber boots, work clothes, jars of very dusty candy. Dried figs and sausages hung from the ceiling. There were slippery grease spots on the floor beneath the sausages.

A very small, very wrinkled man was hidden behind a pile of papers at a desk in the back. He looked surprised to have a customer.

Since we didn't know the word for postcard, my mother drew a rectangle in the air and pretended to write an address on it.

The man looked worried at first. Then he smiled.

The next minute, he pulled a fly swatter from a box under the counter. With a wide grin, he handed it to my mother.

She looked at it, frowned, then tried again. This time she licked an imaginary stamp and put the imaginary postcard in an imaginary mailbox. She started flapping her arms. I guess that was the postcard being flown by carrier pigeon across the Atlantic Ocean.

The man stared at her. Then he slapped the counter with his hand. By some miracle, he understood. He pulled the last two black-and-white postcards on earth from a drawer.

One of them had a picture of a donkey on it. Maybe it was the ear-biting donkey that turned into a lion. The other had a fuzzy picture of fields with stone walls.

Max grabbed the donkey postcard. "Miro loves donkeys."

I wondered how he knew that. There weren't any donkeys in our neighborhood at home.

I ended up with the out-of-focus picture of fields with a heap of rocks that looked like a collapsed pyramid.

We left the store, and I reminded my mother that we needed stamps. She sighed. She was exhausted from playing charades with the man in the store, and now she was going to have to do the same thing in a post office.

It was time to ask Fred for help. He jumped up from his chair, nearly knocking over the old men and their canes.

"Sorry, I forgot all about you guys! Yes, there's a post office here ... in a way. I'd better go with you."

He led Max and me into the village. The main street split into two, and we took the steeper slope toward the top of the village where the church stood.

"We saw this strange woman feeding cats on the dock," I told Fred.

"What's the matter with her?" Max wanted to know. "She yelled at me."

"She doesn't like people looking at her," I said.

"That's only because she doesn't know you," Fred explained. "She's never been off the island. She likes everything to be the same, so when she sees someone new, she gets scared."

"I was scared, too," Max said.

"I don't think she knows how to talk," I added.

"People say she could talk when she was young," Fred told me. "Then something happened to her, but no one really knows what. Everyone has a different idea, but they're all just stories. Some people think she saw something that scared her out of her wits."

"Like a monster?" Max asked.

"Maybe," Fred said. "Anyway, she can't tell us what happened."

Fred stopped to catch his breath on the steep slope. "She won't hurt you. When you see her, just talk the way you would to anyone else."

We walked past gardens and orchards. Everyone was very busy with figs. Ladies were standing on wooden ladders, picking figs from the lower branches of trees. Some of them had climbed onto the higher branches, which couldn't have been easy, since they were wearing long flowered skirts, aprons and heavy rubber boots. The very oldest women, who couldn't climb trees or ladders, were taking figs from baskets and spreading them on wooden racks to dry in the sun.

I didn't see anyone my age. This was an island without roads, and without kids. It was like the island had been invaded by aliens from the Planet of Very Old People.

"These are the best figs in the world," Fred declared, and he stole one off a rack as we walked by.

A woman on a ladder started scolding him. Her voice sounded like fingernails on a chalkboard.

Fred blew her a kiss and popped the fig into his mouth.

"Next time I'll get one for you."

"I don't want an old lady chasing me," Max said.

"Don't worry, they don't run very fast," I told him.

The figs, Fred said, were best when they were fresh. But people here dried them so they could have fruit during the winter. They twisted them into wreaths like the ones you see at Christmas.

We stopped in front of a house. Fred knocked on the heavy wooden door.

Then he opened it and we walked in.

A man was sitting at an ancient rolltop desk, the kind that has a cover on it that slides down. Fred told him what we wanted, and the man opened a dusty leather folder. Inside was something that looked like a stamp collection from the last century.

Welcome to the Vrgada post office!

With trembling hands, the post office man pulled a stamp from his dusty folder with a pair of tweezers. He examined it through a magnifying glass. Then he held out his hand.

"I can't pay him," I told Fred. "I don't have any money."

"Don't worry about money. Just give him the card."

Max and I gave the man our black-and-white postcards. He moistened two stamps on a sponge and stuck them on the cards.

The service was really good here. Where we lived, we had to stick our own stamps on our letters.

The man pointed at what was probably his

dining-room table. Max sat down to write his message to Miro. I wanted to write to Flor, a girl in my class, but I was afraid someone would read what I wrote.

Then I remembered that no one here knew English. That was a relief, for once!

I handed my card to the post-office man. He put it in his shirt pocket and patted it a couple of times. I guess that was the Vrgada mailbox.

"Don't worry," Fred said when we got outside. "It will get to where it's going one of these days."

We walked back to the center of the village. Nothing had changed. Gordana, the queen of Vrgada, was sitting in the middle of a crowd of her admirers. My mother had her sketchbook out again.

I snuck a look. She was drawing the old men with their canes, pipes and sailor caps. Next to them was a sketch of Gordana sitting on a throne with a crown on her head.

## SEVEN
### The Hermit of Urgada

*M*y father always says he likes to get off the beaten track and visit new places. But if you ask me, he was spending more time drinking coffee with Fred in the café than exploring the island.

One day after lunch, even my mother had had enough. She picked up her sketchpad.

"I'm going down to the harbor to draw boats," she announced.

I decided it was time to make my getaway.

Of course, I had to take Max with me.

At the last house at the edge of the village, an old lady was standing on top of a wall. She was picking figs off a tree and putting them in the pockets of her apron.

The old ladies on Vrgada were pretty athletic. I didn't think my grandmother could climb a wall.

We walked past a wheelbarrow filled with figs. I wanted to steal one the way Fred had, but I didn't dare.

As Max and I went by, the lady called to us. I looked up just as she dropped a couple of freshly picked figs in our direction. I caught them before they hit the ground.

"*Hvala,*" I said.

She laughed, as if a foreign kid who could say thank you in her language was the funniest thing in the world. She laughed so hard I thought she would fall off her wall like Humpty Dumpty.

I think I needed a few more words in my vocabulary.

Soon the village was behind us. We ate our figs as we walked down the road that wound through the fields. Clouds of swallows swooped by, chasing insects. Crows flew overhead, cawing loudly.

"Those birds sound like the fish witch," Max said.

"Maybe she's hiding in that cemetery over there. Let's go look."

"No way!"

I pushed open the gate. It made a low creaking noise, like in a horror movie.

Max stopped on the road and crossed his arms. "I'm not going in there!"

I stepped into the cemetery. I wouldn't have done that in the middle of the night, that's for sure.

I looked around and saw something strange.

All the names on the gravestones were the same. It was as if the same person was buried in every grave. A person named Andric.

But how could that be?

Then I remembered Fred saying that everyone was related here. I closed the gate behind me.

As we walked farther into the countryside, I noticed the fields were separated by stone walls. Sometimes the walls ran around a single tree. Oth-

er times they bordered big fields where vegetables grew.

As we walked, the stone walls seemed to grow higher, and the path got narrower. Pretty soon I couldn't see over them. All I could see were the tops of trees.

Why would anyone go to all the trouble of building walls this high? Were they hiding something?

Then more paths split off from ours and ran in different directions, between the same high walls.

"Where do we go now?" Max asked.

"Let's try this way."

Some walls turned circles or led to passages that branched off, then stopped in dead ends.

Suddenly I got the feeling that the walls were part of a labyrinth. But it wasn't the kind of labyrinth you draw on a piece of paper, like a puzzle you have to find your way out of. Here someone had built a maze out of thousands and thousands of stones. And I was in the middle of it.

I wondered if there was a Minotaur in the middle of the maze. You know, the creature that was half man and half bull. Wouldn't it be great to see something like that?

There was only one problem. The Minotaur liked to eat people.

"This place is sort of spooky," Max said.

Maybe he had read my thoughts.

"Okay, we'll go a different way."

I helped Max climb over one of the lower stone walls and we ended up in another passageway. Soon it split in two.

Max stopped. "Now what?"

"Search me."

"I don't like this," he complained. "We might get lost."

After it had eaten a lot of his friends, the guy who conquered the Minotaur brought a ball of string with him so he could find his way out of the labyrinth.

I didn't have any string. I made a little pile of stones in the middle of the intersection so we would know which way the exit was. Then we turned left.

We couldn't really tell where we were going, or where we had come from.

I stopped and listened. The locusts were chirping madly, and the wind whistled in the pine trees. From far away I heard the sound of a boat engine.

We could have been anywhere, or nowhere.

Suddenly I had a funny feeling. Was the path we were following getting narrower? Was someone squeezing us into a funnel?

That didn't make sense. These walls had been here forever. My imagination must have been playing tricks on me.

Next thing we knew, a huge stone wall blocked our way.

Another dead end.

I decided to go back. We stopped at an intersection that I hadn't noticed the first time. The walls seemed to be moving and changing direction.

"Isn't that the little pile of stones you made?" Max asked.

There were millions of stones everywhere. I couldn't tell the difference between one pile and the next. Making a pile of stones to mark the way out wasn't my most brilliant idea.

The sun was getting low in the sky and Max was looking worried.

We walked and walked between the high stone walls. It was like having a dream where you're running but you never get anywhere.

We reached a spot where part of the wall had fallen down. Maybe that was the way out of the maze!

We stepped through the opening.

In a clearing before us stood an old ruined cabin. It reminded me of the wrecked houses we had seen in the divided village.

"It might be booby-trapped," Max whispered.

I took a few careful steps closer. All sorts of tools were hanging on the outside wall of the cabin: rakes and shovels and pitchforks. They were the kinds of tools you might find on a farm, but this was no farm. The only things growing here were rocks.

Something hanging in the trees caught my eye. I moved a little closer. Leaves and branches were woven together into a ball to make something that looked just like a human head. There were dozens of them in every tree.

"What are those things?" Max asked.

"I don't know. Some kind of decoration."

"This place is weird. I don't like it."

I saw something else hanging from a tree. From where I stood, it looked like a rug. Then the wind blew and the rug began to swing. Drops of something dripped onto the grass. The drops were red.

That was no rug.

It was the fur from an animal that had just been killed.

"I think you're right," I said to Max in a low voice. "We'd better go."

We turned and headed for the opening in the wall.

You know that feeling you get when someone is watching you, even when you have your back turned? It's like when you're in school and not paying attention, and all of a sudden you know the teacher has her eye on you?

That's the feeling I had as we moved away from the cabin.

I couldn't stop myself. I turned and looked.

A shadow moved inside the cabin. Then someone stepped into the yard.

It was a man who looked like a scarecrow, with long stringy hair, tattered clothes and dirty bare feet. His eyes glowed in his dark face as if they were on fire. His long beard was full of twigs and leaves. In one hand he was holding the skin of an animal. In the other hand he had a heavy stick.

Max and I stood absolutely still, as if we were hypnotized. We stared at the man.

I had never seen a hermit, but I knew he was one.

Hermits lived on their own, far from other people. And they didn't like visitors.

He bared his teeth at us and took a step in our direction. Then he raised his heavy stick in the air.

He yelled something, but I didn't understand.

I remembered what you were supposed to do when you met a wild animal face to face. You retreated very, very slowly, but you didn't turn your back.

I grabbed Max's hand and started backing away. Max stumbled over a rock, but I kept him from falling.

We inched our way toward the opening in the wall. I kept my eyes on the hermit's face. For every step we took away from him, he took one in our direction.

When we reached the hole in the wall, I pushed Max through and scrambled after him.

"Come on, Max, run!"

We ran as fast as we could down the path, through the giant maze of rocks. I was sure I could hear the hermit's bare feet slapping on the ground, and I wondered what would happen if he caught

us. The bloody animal skin hanging from a tree flashed in my mind.

"Come on, Max! Faster!"

We ran along walls that twisted and turned, trying not to trip on the sharp rocks. We ran and ran until Max started to cry.

I looked behind us. We were alone.

We stopped to catch our breath. I listened for the sounds of someone running. A few locusts were rubbing their wings together, and some seagulls circled overhead, calling to each other. That was all.

We had escaped the hermit. But where were we? I'd been so scared I'd forgotten to keep track of where we were going.

I remembered what I'd thought a few days ago. *Lost, on this tiny island? Impossible!*

"Let's go, Max," I told my little brother. "We have to get out of here."

The sun was setting, and the high stone walls cast long shadows on the path in front of us.

"What if we meet that horrible monster again?" Max asked in a trembling voice. He wouldn't let go of my hand.

"We won't," I said.

"How do you know?"

I thought a few seconds.

"That man was a hermit," I told Max. "Hermits don't like to be around other people."

We kept on walking. I had no idea whether we were getting farther away or closer to the village. It was a desperate feeling.

Finally, Max flopped down on the rocky path.

"I'm too tired. I can't go on."

I sat down next to him. Maybe if I stopped walking and started thinking, I could find some way out of this labyrinth.

When we started out, we had the sun behind us. Now it was disappearing very quickly in front of us.

Did that mean we should turn around and go back the other way, toward the hermit's cabin?

What if he was waiting for us?

I didn't want to think about that.

Then, in the silence, I heard the sound of church bells.

We were saved — saved by the bell! If we followed our ears, the bells would guide us back to the village.

They were still ringing when we spotted the village through the trees. I could see men sitting in front of their houses, watching women push wheelbarrows loaded with figs.

Everything looked normal — as normal as things could be in Vrgada. You couldn't have guessed that nearby, a hermit dressed in rags was hiding in a half-ruined stone cabin.

And where were my parents?

Exactly! They were sitting in the same chairs in front of the café, still talking with Fred and Gordana. And Fred had a cup of coffee in his hand.

It was like stepping out of another dimension and back into the normal world. And no time had passed at all.

I collapsed onto a chair next to my parents.

My mother gave me a long look.

"Did something happen?" she asked. "You look like you saw a ghost."

"No, not a ghost."

"Then what did you see?"

"We saw someone in the woods. I think he was a hermit."

Fred jumped to his feet. "You saw the hermit of Vrgada?"

"You know about him?"

"Where did you see him?"

"We were exploring an old cabin. I turned around and there he was."

"That's amazing," Gordana said. "He never lets anyone see him."

"And no one ever goes to his place," Fred added. "Everyone is too afraid."

"He is pretty scary."

"Did he try and hurt you?" my mother asked.

"He shook his stick at us. He seemed real mad. He yelled something, but I didn't understand."

"You surprised him," Gordana explained. "You probably scared him."

"He wasn't as scared as I was," Max said.

"What is he doing out there?" I asked.

"Actually, he used to live in the village ..." Fred began.

"He was one of us," Gordana added. "But then he signed up to fight in the war, even though he didn't have to."

"And he left his mind there," Fred went on. "He must have seen terrible things, something that pushed him over the edge."

"Like what?" Max whispered, his eyes wide.

"There is nothing but terrible things to see in

a war," Gordana said angrily. "Death and hatred. Neighbors becoming enemies. People with too much power and too many guns ..."

"When he came back to the island, he wouldn't talk to anyone. He moved out to that old ruin and started raising goats. He won't talk to anyone but his animals."

"What about those round things hanging in the trees?" I asked. "Maybe they're some kind of message."

"You're the first person who has seen them," Fred told me. "This island is so full of stories and secrets, it would take a hundred years to figure them all out."

"How can he live out there all by himself?" I wondered.

"People leave food for him," Gordana said.

"They take it to his house?"

"No. They leave it on a rock someplace, not far from his house. No one ever goes to his cabin."

"That's nice of people to do that," my mother said.

"They feel that whatever happened to him, it was a little bit their fault, too," Gordana explained. "Because of the war."

The next day, I headed out to the labyrinth again with a bag of chocolate bars. With Fred's help, I had

bought every chocolate bar in the village store. I figured people would bring the hermit fruit or bread,
but no one would think of leaving him chocolate.

If I lived in a labyrinth made of rocks with only
goats and bad memories to keep me company, I'd
like to have a chocolate bar once in a while.

The hermit of Vrgada wouldn't know they came
from me, but that didn't matter.

I knew.

# EIGHT
## Goodbye to the Wheelbarrows

The next day, I snuck out early in the morning before Max or anyone else woke up. I wanted to go out by myself for once. I wanted to get away from the circus.

I walked along the rocky shore and around the harbor, where the fishermen's nets were drying. I started climbing a steep path that wound through the woods. I followed it down a cliff, all the way to a deserted beach of white sand that shimmered in the sunlight.

Tall red cliffs rose above the beach. Trees leaned over the edge, barely hanging on by their roots. Hawks rode the wind currents high in the sky, looking for something to eat.

There wasn't even a fishing boat on the horizon.

I felt a little like Robinson Crusoe as I waded into the clear warm water. Small silvery fish swam away from my shadow.

Robinson Crusoe would have made a spear from a branch, or woven a basket out of seagrass to catch them. Though it would have taken a lot of those skinny fish to make a good meal.

Imagine living for years and years all alone, surviving on fish and coconuts. I like being alone and doing what I want, but living on a desert island would be really hard. No one to talk to, no one to tell you stories, nothing to read, no music ...

It would drive me crazy.

But I didn't have to worry about being alone too long. The peace and quiet was broken by loud whooping noises as the Traveling Circus appeared at the top of the cliff. Max was waving his arms and yelling as he ran down the path. My father and Fred were lugging a huge picnic basket. Behind them, Gordana and my mom were loaded down with towels, hats and a beach umbrella. They all were waving as if we hadn't seen each other for years.

As I watched them making their way down the path, out of the corner of my eye I saw something move in the forest above. I wondered if it was the hermit spying on us from his shadow world, telling his goats about the nosy people who didn't under-

stand that the war was still going on in his mind.

Then the shadow disappeared.

Max landed in a spray of sand at my feet.

"What are you doing here? How come you went off all alone? I was looking everywhere for you."

I was just taking a Robinson Crusoe break from you, I thought. But I didn't bother telling him that. He wasn't listening anyway.

We sat in the shade of the beach umbrella. Gordana started passing out the food.

My mother sighed happily. "This has been a wonderful trip! We never would have discovered this beautiful place if it weren't for you."

"It's even better than how you described it the first time," my father said.

"How did you and Fred meet?" I asked.

"Your father was wandering around a book fair in Montenegro, looking lost," Fred said.

He did that all the time, I thought.

"And I helped him find his way. We became friends and promised we'd stay in touch and meet again."

"Like Libero and me."

"Exactly. But the war wrecked our plans. No one could travel here anymore. And besides, I was caught in the middle, between the two sides. I was living in Croatia, but I'm from Serbia. Before, it didn't matter because we were all one country. But when the country split up and everyone started fighting each other, Serbia turned into the enemy here."

He pointed to the calm blue sea and the small sailboat drifting by.

"Can you imagine a war here? And with me as the enemy?"

On a day like this, it really was hard to imagine. But when I remembered the village where we had stopped, with half the houses destroyed, and the other half in perfect shape, anything seemed possible.

"I promised myself," Fred went on, "that once everything was peaceful again, I would invite you to come for vacation, so you could see how beautiful this country is."

"It sure took you a long time!" Gordana said, waving her finger at my parents.

"That's because they lost your postcard," I told her. "If I hadn't found it under the stove, we never would have come."

"What were you doing under the stove?" Gordana asked.

"That's a long story."

Max jumped up. "I'm going for a swim!"

He made a run for the water. I went in after him.

As Max pretended to be a shark, I floated on my back and looked up at the sky. Gordana said the war had never come to Vrgada, but that wasn't completely true. Maybe no one ever fired a gun here, but the shadow of the war was everywhere. And I had seen it.

At home, a lot of my friends talk about their grandfathers. A grandfather is someone you can do things with that you can't do with your father. You can say things to your grandfather that you can't say to your parents.

I never had a grandfather. Mine died a long time ago, before I was born.

I decided I would adopt Fred as my grandfather. First of all, he was a great storyteller. He had an adventurous life in a country that survived a war. And he wasn't afraid to talk about what had happened here.

Otherwise the secret stories of Vrgada would have stayed secret.

And I would have never known any of them.

## THE END

MARIE-LOUISE GAY is a world-renowned author and illustrator of children's books. She has been nominated for the Hans Christian Andersen Award and has two Governor General's awards to her credit. She is best known for her Stella and Sam books, which have been published in more than fifteen languages. Her most recent book is *Any Questions?*

Born and raised in Chicago, DAVID HOMEL is an award-winning novelist, screenwriter, journalist and translator. He is a two-time winner of the Governor General's Award for translation, and the author of ten novels, including *The Speaking Cure* (winner of the Hugh MacLennan Prize and the Jewish Public Library Award for fiction) and, most recently, *The Fledglings*.

Marie-Louise and David live in Montreal.

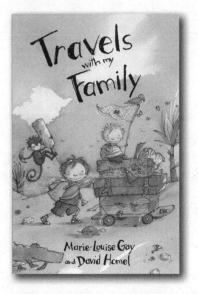

TRAVELS WITH MY FAMILY

Family vacations are supposed to be something to look forward to.

Unless, that is, your parents have a habit of turning every outing into a risky proposition. By accident, of course.

So instead of dream vacations to Disney World and motels with swimming pools, Charlie's parents are always looking for that out-of-the-way destination where other tourists don't go. The result? Eating grasshoppers in Mexico, forgetting the tide schedule while collecting sand dollars off the coast of Georgia, and mistaking alligators for logs in the middle of Okefenokee Swamp.

"... it has the ring of truth for anyone who has ever been forced to spend long hours in the back seat of a car."
— *Los Angeles Times*

## ON THE ROAD AGAIN!

Charlie's family is on the road again — this time to spend a year in a tiny village in southern France.

They experience the spring migration of sheep up to the mountain pastures and the annual running of the bulls (in which Charlie's father is trapped in a phone booth by a raging bull). Most of all, though, Charlie and his little brother, Max, grow fond of their new neighbors — the man who steals ducks from the local river, the dog who sleeps right in the middle of the street, and their friends Rachid and Ahmed, who teach them how to play soccer in the village square.

"… full of good humour … this novel will hit a home run …" — *Globe and Mail*

## Summer in the City

Charlie can't wait for school to be over. But he's wondering what particular vacation ordeal his parents have lined up for the family this summer. Canoeing with alligators in Okefenokee? Getting caught in the middle of a revolutionary shootout in Mexico? Perhaps another trip abroad?

Turns out, this summer the family is staying put, in their hometown — Montreal, Canada. A "staycation," his parents call it.

Charlie is doubtful at first but, in the end, decides that there may be adventures to be had in his own neighborhood.

"An upbeat summer idyll likely to draw chuckles whether read alone or aloud." — *Kirkus*